I0748423

The Corazón Treasure

An Ozarks Adventure
for Lost Souls
and Spanish Silver!

By Kory Umlauf

Kory@KoryUmlauf.com

Ordering Information:
Quantity sales. Special discounts are available on quantity purchases by corporations, associations, and others. For details, contact the "Special Sales Department" at the email address above.

The Corazon Treasure/ Kory Umlauf. - 1st edition.
ISBN 978-0-578-82153-5

This book is dedicated with infinite love to my sons
Blake & Grant Umlauf

Provision Mapping

Your dreams written down with details becomes your life's map. All great adventures require a map, provisions, and bold persistence to challenge the obstacles along the trail. So, dream big, always carry a map, plan your provisions, choose an experienced guide and reliable companions, be prepared to make your own trail, and remember dreams are better when achieved together!"

–Kory Umlauf

Published by Provision Mapping LLC

Contents

CHAPTER ONE

Baseball, Brotherhood and the Battlefield

Step up to the plate is a term I have heard often, but to take that confident walk to the diamond makes me realize how much baseball is like real life. All too often we randomly swing at everything thrown our way with the hopes that we'll finally connect to a purpose, only to send us running with passion from base to base remembering that there's nothing more important than the ultimate goal of making it back home safe.

My Dad always tells me I'm a great player with a lion heart! He tells me that I'm a natural leader with a fierce competitive spirit; I understand what it means because I feel it run deep through into my soul. It was always a joy to have him there to watch me take the swing for the fences. I'm still not sure if I was born this way or if it is skills molded from the protective lessons and fast balls of life thrown at me by my big brother, Caleb. One thing is certain, I had become a force to be reckoned with, and we both made our Coach the proudest father on the planet.

It always started with me slowly digging my spikes into the loose dirt grooves left by the batters to get my stance just right; my muscles tightened as I lifted my bat in the air twirling it in small circles, then with a firm grip and a determined lip I turned my head towards the pitcher with a stare and a nod as if to say, "I'm here and I'm ready - give me your best and I'll show you what I'm made of." I tried to make my confidence and willpower glow visibly around my body. The pitcher tried to make his best, "I'm tough" face, but I didn't find it amusing enough to flinch; in fact, if I moved at all it was to raise the bat a little higher. With a breath and stretch the ball left the formidable opponent's hand and flew across the plate so low the dust tried to run away as the catcher scooped it up and threw it back to the pitcher, who was admiring the sneers and jeers that came from the players around him. It didn't matter much to us who the other team was, what they said, or where they were from. Our creed was to always play with all our hearts and souls, with a strong moral character of respect toward others.

But as the pitcher became still and looked down at the ball everyone became quiet again and waited to watch the ensuing battle. I was also a pitcher so I saw every move in slow motion as I followed that ball straight to my bat; and this one just hit the sweet spot. I'm not sure exactly how that term got started but when it hit just right, it would most certainly make the sweetest sound ever. The whole team was yelling from the dugout - Cole, Casey, Luke, Garth, TJ, Mark and, Michael, all hollering a cheer that could probably be heard from the next county. By the time we saw the ball hit the ground I had already rounded first base. Big brother Caleb was the base coach, and with a prideful grin from ear to ear he waved me onto second. The ball had been scooped up and was on its way to second, as well, but I could slide like a freight train. As the dust cleared, I would be standing on the base like I had walked there.

Brock was in the batter's circle, and we all knew what was next. He had proven many times that he would always get us home. His mother Kayla was at every game and loved him with all that was in her; to this day she holds the title for the loudest mom in the stands. To the best of my recollection, the team was my Dad's idea; he was frustrated with the nepotism that sometimes takes place on teams coached by fathers, so he told me to make a list of my friends who had a love for playing the game. We held practice on an old farm down a county road. A wealthy man had put in a small ball field for his son to practice on, and he'd since gone off to college leaving our team blessed with a great place to meet, learn, and grow. One day, in the middle of workouts, Caleb was soft-tossing a few in the batting cage to Lucas and TJ while Dad was hitting balls to Garth, Rhett, and Michael. Stephen would catch and toss him the returns for the next drill, when seemingly out of nowhere Cole is standing next to Dad and says, "Hey, Coach! This is my friend Brock, and he wants to play on our team."

Dad took a puzzled look around and quickly deduced he wasn't old enough to drive; there wasn't a car or bike in sight. After a polite, "hello, Brock, nice to meet you," he had to ask, "where did you come from?" Brock pointed to a dirt road down the street and said, "just down there a bit." Then he explained that he really loved baseball and would do anything if he could be part of our team and play with us. As it turned out, we had two spots to fill, so circumstance and the way he looked at Dad with those lost puppy-dog eyes, we all knew he was already one of us. I wasn't sure where we would find the next player, but it seemed as though fate or something was writing a plan for us. That evening, the phone rang from a father who had heard about us. He promised my Dad that his son would be a great addition to our team, so Luke met us at the next practice. When we saw the kind strength in his soul, we knew he would become a great friend. It had to work for good as we had already put his name on the roster! Little did I know then that our little team of friends would have an incredible adventure that would change our lives forever.

"Good game Brock!"

We greeted coach and my bro's with a chorus line of high fives to the sound of cheering parents as they headed back to the dugout to get ready for the team-talk! Winning with my friends is an amazing feeling that fills my heart with joy.

The only thing that could make us happier is if Dad tells one of his silly baseball jokes like Why do we always sing "Take Me Out To The Ball Game" when we're already there?" or the time he told us about a group of kids who was playing in a farm field, and one of them hit a chicken with a baseball and then proceeded to yell, Fowl ball!" The last time he told us that story with his serious coach face we rolled in the grass laughing so hard Cole peed in his pants. Just the thought could make Brock smile; clearly he needs to. As Dad told us all how proud he was of our character I noticed Brock was staring at the ground as if to be carrying the weight of the world on his shoulders. On the way to the car, he asked if we could meet at the clubhouse tomorrow as he desperately needed our help.

CHAPTER TWO

Legends from the Heart

It was a long night, with many wandering thoughts about what it was Brock needed my help with. Not knowing how long we would be gone, I stuffed some peanut butter roll-up sandwiches and chocolate chip cookies into my pack, grabbed a jug of juice and headed out the door and down the trail. With school and baseball, it had been a few days since I'd seen the club. Grandpa had helped us build it: called "the clubhouse," it's actually a three-walled tree shed with a view of a small, wet-weather creek. It sits in the fork of a huge oak tree that looks like a big hand holding a box in the air. It has an old wood ladder attached to the side, with a rope so we can hoist up the ladder and lay it sideways across the floor of the open section. This keeps any unwanted visitors from getting up the tree, and makes a gate which keeps us from rolling out if and when we are asleep. The relaxing sound of the water cascading down the creek below combined with the rustling cymbals that the wind makes with the tree as the leaves dance against the sky's sparkling blue dance floor added to the beautiful melodic chirps from the Cardinals and Sparrows; the tree shed quickly becomes a place where everyone feels at peace. Must be why we catch Dad napping here all the time. As I crested the hill and looked down the path, there were two does standing guard over a snow-spotted fawn. They're usually eating from the blackberry patch and probably heard the crunching ground cover beneath my feet.

As they bounced away across the ridge with their tails waving white surrender flags, I remembered stories my grandpa told us about why they have a hunting season (to keep the population under control from disease). Like him, though, I think I would rather watch than hunt them - especially when you see the little ones. Besides, I'm certain my girlfriend Maya would not like it, as she sleeps, eats, and dreams all day about puppies and babies. What an incredibly beautiful girl she is - inside and out. I was happy to meet Brock to see what he wants, but I really miss Maya and can't wait to see her again.

When I got to the clubhouse Brock was already there and Cole was with him. They had a secret back pathway from Cole's house, so I wasn't surprised aside from that they beat me there.

"Hey Gage!"

"Hi Brock, Suup Cole? This must be good as you're rarely on time."

Cole chuckled, but then again he usually does. The only thing bigger than Cole's funny bone is his stomach. He's a jovial character that always sees the humorous side of everything, and he could make Brock laugh on cue. But this time Brock looked serious. Before I could even ask, Brock said;

"OK guys, here's the deal. You remember that story Mr. Stewart told us about the Spaniard Desoto's Lost Treasure?"

"Yeaaah?"

I stretched the word in wonder as to where he was going with this question.

"The Corazon Treasure that promised crazy wild riches beyond belief and immortality forever?"

"Yes, that one!" Brock said with excitement. "I need to find it..."

I beat Cole to the punchline this time and we both laughed hysterically with the same responses "It's beyond belief."

"It's not funny this time, guys," Brock said. We paused as he lowered his head and stared at the ground below and with a solemn soft voice he explained, "It's my mom, she needs heart surgery, and I must find it to save her."

Tears crept into his eyes, "you guys know I have no father, and I don't know what I would possibly do without my mom. She always told me that we must look out for each other. It's my responsibility. I have to fix this and the only way is to find the Treasure so she can have a new heart and immortality against death!"

"Do you really believe that, Brock? Maybe the teacher was using a wild story as a way to keep us interested in the history lesson."

"YES!" exclaimed Brock with a snarled lip that soon became a frown. "I have to! It's my only hope and I need your help."

"The riches would certainly be cool, too," said Cole.

We all sat silently and tried to imagine what it would be like to be so rich and live forever. It didn't take long before Cole lifted his head, rolled his shoulders back and stated with determination, "Let's do it!"

"What do we have to lose?" I said.

"My mom," was Brock's quick reply.

"Ok, I'm in."

"Where do we start? Do we tell my Dad?"

"Nooo, not yet," said Brock. "You guys don't even believe it yet, so let's not go telling everyone. They might tell us we're silly and not help. Besides, I don't want anyone to know about my mom and how scared I am."

"Alright guys, we're a team."

"Yeah, and if we find it we're a very rich team," said Cole.

"That'd be cool," I said as we all chuckled together.

"Well, first we have to find a map."

"How do we do that?"

"Mr. Stewart would tell us to go to the library and study."

"Oh, man, are you serious?"

"How many times are you going to ask me that?"

"Yes, this is very serious!" said Brock. "Now let's get going."

Cole looked over at my backpack with a raised eyebrow and said, "hey, since we're a team and sharing everything, how 'bout showing me some love with one of those sandwiches I know you've got stashed in there?"

"Cole!"

"Listen guys, I'm more than willing to go on an adventure, but there is no sense in starving while we do it."

Laughing was good for Brock, so we climbed down, split the sandwiches and ate them while walking so we could keep everybody happy. We headed back up the trail to my house. It would be easy to get my Dad to take us to the library; he goes there all the time.

Dad looked at us with a wrinkled forehead of confused pride (with the hint of a suspicious grin) as he grabbed the keys and told us to saddle up. Once we arrived we left him browsing the music CD's, and headed for the historical archives for our proverbial homework project.

"Hey Brock, since we really have no idea what we're looking for, let's ask the lady at the help desk."

"Thanks Gage - after a barrage of questions from the mad librarian Ms. Adtussen, here we sit with a bunch of books full of stories about Spain's conquest of the Americas and \still no idea how to find a treasure."

"And just like Stewie she keeps looking at us to see what we're doing."

"Stewie?" asked Cole.

"You know, Mr. Stewart, our teacher."

"Shhh, don't laugh, Cole! See, she's looking over here again."

Brock suddenly leaned into the book and pointed to a page. "Check this out guys. It says here that DeSoto was chased north by 200 Indian warriors from the richest province of the cacique of Aquixo - or present day Arkansas - so this shows he really was in the Ozarks."

"Duh," said Cole. "That's what Stewie told us in class."

"Yeah, and I heard the same story about Spanish treasure when my Mom and Dad took me to Silver Dollar City and we went through the Marvel Cave."

"I have been there, too. It's super cool!"

"Yeah, caves are always cool because they're underground," said Cole with his head buried in his phone.

We both called out "Cole" at the same time and gave him the same look the librarian was giving us.

"Ok, I know, I'll get serious."

"He also said that back then you wouldn't have had state lines, so southwest Missouri and northwest Arkansas were and still are technically the same Ozark region."

Gage lifted his book and turned to us, reading. "A large party of Spaniards mining for gold and silver built a large log fortress on Bread Tray Mountain near the mouth of the James River, where it flows into the White river. They found a cave full of silver ore. The Indians were told he was the 'Child of the Sun,' so they followed his guidance. But he mistreated them until they rebelled and fought back, and many died, including DeSoto. Right before he died he appointed Captain Luis de Moscoso Alvarado. It says he was a good leader and got frustrated with all the wars with the Indians, so they headed south to Mexico. If the treasure was left behind in quick retreat, then it really could be somewhere near there as they departed the Ozarks."

I didn't think Brock was listening, but he was already looking up Bread Tray Mountain on the White River.

"Check this out, it's on Table Rock Lake."

I looked over and when I saw it my eyes widened.

"Guys, I know where that is. It's real close to Clearwater Cove - you know, the Young Life camp Caleb went to last summer."

"Let's go look for clues!" Brock yelled with excitement.

"Oh no, now you've done it, here she comes."

Ms. Adtussen stood at the end of the table with her arms folded, glaring at us over the top of her glasses. "My little Chris has told me about you boys, so I suspected you might cause trouble. Now listen to me very carefully, this is your last warning. Keep quiet or you're out of here."

"Yes, Ma'am," we all moaned softly.

As she turned and walked away. holding her head high as if proud of her presumed authority, Cole looked at us with a puzzled snarl and said, "Chris who?"

"You know that skinny kid with the screechy voice from Mr. Reyes' class? I think that's his mom."

"Oh, now it makes sense!"

"What does?"

"Why he's so loud. He probably gets shushed all the time at home."

We all snickered as quietly as we could, and slid out of our chairs to go find Dad.

"We gotta find a way to get to Bread Tray Mountain and look for clues."

"Yes, Brock, we'll figure out a way."

"Look," said Cole. "There's Lil' Loud Chris hiding behind that bookcase. What's he doing? There's no test here, so no need to cheat."

"I bet he's just not allowed to get that far from his momma."

We all got a kick outta that - even Brock!

"Let's go stand by your dad so he'll leave us alone."

"Hey Coach, what did you find?"

"I was about to ask you guys the same thing."

"Check this out, I found Jeremy Camp, Big Daddy Weave and Mercy Me."

He paused and then asked the question we've heard more than once: "Why is Cole snickering at me?"

"It's cool Coach, do they have any 'Gangsta Rap'?"

"Stop it Brock! Let me show you some real music, See this? Otis Redding - he had 'Respect' before Arethra and 'Papa's Got a Brand-New Bag' way before the godfather of soul James Brown. And the Rolling Stones got plenty of 'Satisfaction' from your grandparents' radio songs."

"Sheesh, Brock, why did you get my Dad started? He'll go on for days about how we're all brothers from another mother and all new music is the same old beats that have been played before, but with new rebellious words to divide us."

Just then Coached piped up, "how about you let papa get a brand new bag of books and hip hop outta here to the truck, then we'll roll home for some sweet satisfaction at the swimming hole?"

"Stop, Dad."

I was always interested in Dad's stories but never really understood because I had not lived them. But in true lion heart character I would certainly challenge him to see truth in a real way.

CHAPTER THREE

A Wild Ride

Once back at the clubhouse we could devise a plan to go on an adventure and search for the treasure.

"What's your idea, Brock?"

"We'll ride our bikes to Ozark. There are always buses and trucks there headed to Branson."

"Ok, cool idea, but do we tell my Dad?"

"We'll tell him we are going camping."

"But he'll want to go with us."

"Yes, but we'll say that we're going with Cole's family."

"But what about Cole's family. What will we tell them?"

"Chill!" exclaimed Gage, "we trust each other because we never lie. Are you asking me to lie to my Father? He will know by the look on my face and the beads of sweat on my forehead!"

"Please," snarled Brock, "stop with the 'my Dad this' and 'my Dad that.' I'm doing this to save my mom, not for any

Father. Now, let's go find this treasure and everyone will be proud of us when we do."

It was a quiet ride to the restaurant as our minds were spinning with crazy thoughts about this adventure. If we didn't find it, we would all be in huge trouble. As usual, the cars, trucks and buses lined the parking lots.

"You know we should get a job at that restaurant. We could throw those rolls all day long."

"Yea, and it wouldn't suck to eat there every day."

"Cole, do you ever think about anything else but food?"

"Hey look, see that big boat?"

"Yea, don't get distracted again, Cole. We're trying to catch a ride."

"That's just it. The truck pulling that boat says 'Marina Kimberling City.'"

We rolled up to the back side, and I jumped in.

"Hand me my bike."

Before we knew it, we all were laying in the floor of the boat looking at each other with the surreal surprise that this might actually work. All of a sudden, we heard voices getting closer, then car doors closing. We both quickly reached over and put one of our hands over Cole's mouth. and the other with our finger to our lips trying quietly to keep him from yelling as we knew what was coming. When we heard the truck doors close it looked as if his eyes were about to pop out of his head. Once the engine roared and we started moving, we all felt the same scary feeling as there was no turning back.

"Cole! Put the phone down. This is no time for a selfie."

It seemed like an exceptionally long time of listening to the change in the engine as the truck pulled us up and down the highway hills toward Branson. We then felt everything slow and the boat seemed to sway back and forth as we started down some twisting turning roads. The driver must have been tired - when we finally stopped, he didn't even take the trailer off the truck. The noise of closing doors in the dark followed by silence was eerie, so I carefully peeked over the edge of the boat. With our hearts racing, we jumped out, threw our bikes over, and pedaled away like we were in a BMX race. Once we made it far enough away to feel safe, Cole let out a rebel yell that you could hear all the way across the lake!

"What the heck, you been holding that in since we got in the boat?"

Their smiles diminished quickly when I said, "Now what?"

"Well, we made it this far without getting in trouble, so let's ride over to that campground and find a place to crash. Then we'll ride to Bread Tray Mountain in the morning."

"Hey, look at this. Someone must have just left this site - they left wood by the picnic table and the coals are still hot."

"Let's get a fire going. I'm a little cool after that long evening boat ride."

"I'm always cool!" Brock smirked. "I do greatly appreciate your friendship and will show it when I give you guys your 10% cut."

Even Cole was too tired to laugh or argue. Or maybe he was just in a trance staring at the flickering flames. There's something about staring into a campfire. I think I slept with one eye open - it was not near the comfort or safety of knowing my Father is near. I almost hit my head on the tree when Brock grabbed my arm.

"Wake up guys, Look!"

The sky was just starting to get light, he pointed to the table where a young raccoon was looking for breakfast, when he saw us he quickly scampered across the grass and climbed the tree next to us. We felt a little unsure of each other's intentions then he paused and looked right at us. His eyes seemed so kind, it was as if he wanted to say hello and ask for a little snack. Then Brock quietly spoke.

"Do you think he knows where his Father is?"

"A better question might be do you think his parents know where he is?" Replied Gage.

"The Camp Snack Bandit" by Kory Umlauf

The fire had smoldered to nothing, and we lay there in the grass using our backpacks as pillows, watching him watch us and dreaming about our dry warm beds at home. Well, I was, anyway. I'm pretty sure Brock was dreaming about the Corazon treasure. And Cole, well you know...breakfast? That's when I saw the park ranger truck heading straight toward us. We got up and were getting our bikes as he stopped, rolled down his window, and leaned out on his arm. He said, "You boys from that big tent group down by the water?"

"Uh, yeah! That's us," said Brock without blinking an eye.

"Your dads know you're out wandering around this early in the morning?"

"Uh, he will as soon as he quits snoring. Then we'll finally get some sleep."

The ranger chuckled and said, "you boys be sure to follow the park rules, and don't feed my little buddy in that tree, he's getting plump from looking sad and begging for junk food all over this campground. Be careful and have a good day." As he drove off, we all sighed, looked at Brock and thought, "will we ever trust you again?"

"You seem to be really good at this lying thing."

"Is it lying if it helps someone and hurts nobody?"

"That's a good question that I'll be happy to discuss once we aren't being chased." We pedaled up the path to the road and headed for the highway.

We picked up speed once we headed down the hill to the long steel bridge that spanned across the lake. The sun was beginning to rise, and glistened with sparkles on the water. I was grateful it was early - the road narrowed, and there sure wasn't much room for our bikes and passing cars. However, I wasn't looking forward to that huge hill that lay ahead. And here we go - there will be times I want to get off and push but when there's three of us, you never want to be the first one so slow as it goes. Just as it seemed to go on forever, we finally saw a "Lampe, MO" sign ahead that gave us a little boost of much-needed energy. Turning past an old café, it was all back downhill again, with plenty twists and turns. We eventually made it to the Clearwater Cove entrance, so we knew we were close. We did get a glimmer of hope when we saw a sign that read "Bread Tray Mountain Rd." But finding nothing but fields, trees, and scattered houses, we realized this was like looking for a needle in a haystack. Riding up and down and round every path I could feel muscles in my legs I didn't know were there. We parked at the edge of a wooded area, and walked toward a bluff. We could try and imagine where the White and James Rivers merged before the lake was there. Coming across two huge rocks we stood almost in shock that we had travelled so far on a story with no real idea where we were.

"Hey, look at this! These big flat rocks seem to be laid end to end in the ground, almost as if they were a foundation."

"Maybe, I said, "but I think our imaginations are getting the best of us."

"Maybe it's biking up the big hill without having anything to eat."

"Yesss!" Said Cole. "Can we please go back up to that café at the top of the hill and eat some breakfast?"

"I'm with Cole, it's time to stop and work on a better plan. Let's sit for a minute and get ready for the ride back up."

It took much longer to get up the hill than it did to roll down it. We finally pulled into the restaurant, and when we stepped off our bikes the ground seemed to shake below us as our legs adjusted to standing again.

CHAPTER FOUR

Wrinkled Wisdom

It seemed so friendly at the restaurant we didn't take time to lock our bikes. There was a table with a grandpa drinking coffee near the window, and his warm friendly smile made us feel safe.

"Seems like everyone here is so happy," said Brock.

We all agreed. The Ozark mountain air must do something to calm their spirit. Cole looked up from the menu and said, "I'm spending my last penny here. Chicken fried steak with gravy, sunny side up farm fresh Eggs, crispy hash browns and buttermilk biscuits. Is this heaven?"

"I'm having pancakes with peanut butter slathered with maple syrup and a big ole' side of bacon... bacon makes everything better!"

Brock was quiet as he kept his eyes on the menu as if staring straight through it, and with a deep sigh his shoulders dropped and seemed to drag us all down with him.

"My dad says..." I paused. "Well, our Coach says: you've got to step up to the plate with purpose, and it's only the first strike, so learn something from it and get ready for the second pitch!"

"Yeah, I know, it's just...my last hope is to find this treasure and I'm running out of time."

The older men had stopped talking, and when I turned around, one of them was looking right at us. He had long gray hair that draped across his broad shoulders and seemed to wrap all the way around his face with a long bushy matching beard. The coffee cup seemed to steam up from the grip of his strong wrinkled hands. He smiled at us and with a soulful voice said,

"I'm certain time is something you have a lot more of than we do. Don't take it for granted."

He looked down at his cup then back over at us. "We heard you mention treasure. You boys wouldn't be one of those silver treasure hunters, would ya?"

Brock looked over and said, "why? Can you help us?"

He leaned over and extended his strong dark, wrinkled hand that seems to swallow Brock's. "The name's MacArthur. You know, like General Douglas MacArthur, but my good friends call me Mack!"

By the time the waitress got to the table with our food, there wasn't much left for Brock to tell them. You could see them often tear up and lightly smile at their own thoughts as he shared his story about his mom. Mr. MacArthur looked at us and with a kind cool voice and said, "eat your breakfast boys, and I'll tell you a little story."

We ate and listened while he told us his version of the treasure story that the locals had shared for years.

"Boys, we agree about the De Soto story of travels through these hills. My military studies make me think there is great evidence of at least a lookout fortress above the James and White River confluence. This would have had absolutely the best views of possible attacks as well as good exit strategies on two rivers. It also helps to know that this old highway out front is called the old game trail."

"The what?" we both asked.

"Think about terrain, boys. If you were traveling through these hills many years before roads and before man had made wagon trails, where do you think you would have found a clear space to pull wagons without cutting trees and brush all day?"

"Where?"

"Buffalo!"

We all stopped chewing long enough to look up and stare with amazement.

"The buffalo came up this old game trail in giant herds and would have crossed the river. As they did so they would have a left a clearing of brush that would have been easy to follow. Makes sense, right?"

We all nodded.

"So you see, that adds the reason why they would have traveled right across this mountain. And had a travel and escape route with the rivers on the other side. And you know the Spanish treasure story, lead mining, and millions of tourists who have been through the old Marvel Cave back when it was called Marble Cave. I tell you this so you'll consider how many years have passed and how many people since the Spaniards left have travelled and lived in these hills. It may help to consider another story that is more recent, and possibly connected: the Yocum Silver Dollars."

He had our undivided attention. For this elder man to share his time and stories with us was a true gift just by itself. You could see beautiful stories of experience in the wrinkles in his forehead.

"Go ahead, please!"

He leaned back, lifted his mug, and nodded to the waitress for more coffee.

"After the war of 1812, the Delaware Indians became part of the trans-migration, landing most of them in the James River area around 1820. They were joined by Shawnee, Kickapoo, Potawatomi, and Seneca from the East. About the same time, James Yocum of Kentucky moved his family to trap and eventually farm corn, squash, and raise herds of cattle and horses on the banks of the river that some locals would argue is his namesake. It is more than likely, however, that it was named after the James River in Virginia near the early settlement of Jamestown and some lost colonies like Roanoke. That has a great history of how we truly all became Americans together, and has been recently discovered by National Geographic Geno Project - how and why we all share DNA strands from migration back to Africa. But that's another story for another day."

Gage looked at all of us and said, "see, my Dad always says we're brothers from another mother."

Brock looked at Gage with frustration, then Mr. MacArthur continued: "My apologies, I digress. Anyway, while trading, Yocum noticed the Delaware had very high-quality silver in their long beaded necklaces and jewelry. They had learned about a cave from the original Choctaw tribe left by the Spaniards that had silver bars stacked as high as your shoulder. This remained secret for years until the Indians moved west to reservations in Oklahoma. Upon departure they tell about how the Yocum's showed up with gifts of blankets, food, and horses to help with their journey. This is when he learned about the location of the cave and agreed to keep it secret - and take it to the grave. They would be gone travelling for 3 days and return with silver, and using blacksmith tools, they melted ingots and made dies, rolled out sheets and made their own coins.

On one side they stamped "Yocum" and the date "1822," and on the other, "United States of America" and "1 Dollar."

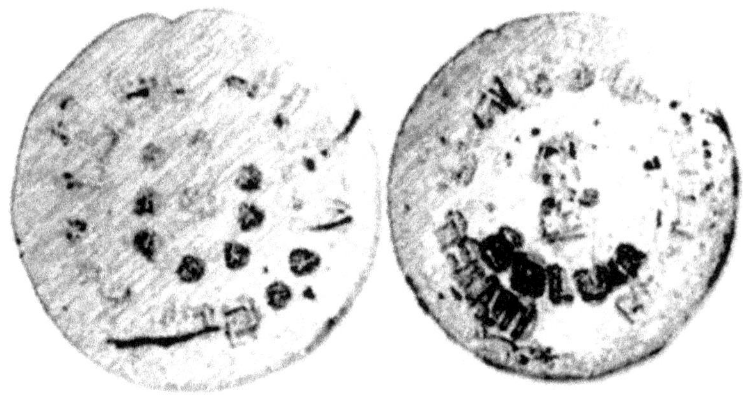

The waitress came to pick up our plates and was smiling, so he paused his story and we thought, "can this be true?" As she left, he looked at us, and we looked at each other and the doubt in our eyes must have been obvious. He glanced back our way after a sip and exclaimed,

"you can prove all this from the history of our government if you don't believe me." He grinned as if he could read our minds.

"No please go ahead, your wisdom is amazing."

He continued, and we were spellbound. "As they began using them to trade furs and goods around the Ozarks, Old Man Gilliss managed the James Fork Trading Post and declared them as very fine silver. He gladly accepted them, so they soon became more available than government-issued money. All was well until surveying crews from a government agency came to issue land to the settlers. They learned about the coins and would not take them, citing an 1833 regulation. There are many long stories about the agents who stopped them from being produced, but James never told them where the cave was. There are just as many stories about where they went, some say they loaded up and disappeared to the wild mountains of Colorado, or went searching for gold in California. I believe they may be buried somewhere near here, as most men I've ever known choose money even if it means their life. My dad's old friend Homer told him stories about his Grandfather Jefferson Johnson, who ran with Jacob Levi Yocum and how they found barrels of his family's silver coins. Add the legend of the man from St. Louis who found a cache near Branson, and you can go on for hours with all the legends of tall tales."

Just then Brock looked like he was going to throw up with the thought that he was losing his dream. Mr. Mack looked at him and shocked us when he said, "keep your eyes on the ball, Brock. There's still hope as I have an idea, and I think you boys may have the mustard to pull this off. You see, I greatly appreciate you boys showing interest in an old man. My days of adventure are long over, and my days can get mighty lonely. Seeing you friends looking out for each other and being respectful to me is why I want to tell you more. You see, my grandfather, who was born in Little Rock, Arkansas, traveled the world as a general for the Army. It is men like him as to why we are free. His outstanding leadership performance built many great American soldiers and was based on the credo of 'Duty. Honor. Country.' This is a trait not seen as often these days. I see this potential in you boys. Do me a favor, and when you have more time someday, read about what it means to be a servant leader. And boys, please remember there are still outlaws and bushwackers in some of the woods of this world. And demanding a safe space is the first clue you haven't learned anything from our ancestors, whose safe space might have been a foxhole so you could have freedom. That said, it's easy to see that everyone you meet just might appear to have good intentions on the outside yet actually have a dark or hurting heart. If so, learn to avoid temptation. Don't follow them, instead lead. Choose life and live it fully every day! It's always a choice: my personality, my habits, even my speech, is a combination of the books I chose to read. The people I choose to listen to, and the thoughts I still choose to tolerate in my mind. Sure, I've made mistakes, many of them, we all have and probably always will. It's the intention of the heart that matters more than the outcome! If you fall, and you might...in fact, you probably will. Don't let that stop you from trying, get up, brush off the dust and keep going. Pursue your dream with Persistence!"

The waitress came over with our check and we thought, "wait, were not ready to go yet. He's about to get to the good stuff."

He looked at us and said, "hang on to your britches, we'll go sit on the porch and finish talking." We each stood up, and started to dig out and combine our money to pay when Mr. MacArthur told the cashier, "these boys are on me, just tell me what I owe for both tables."

They smiled at him, straightened their shoulders, stood at attention and said, "yes sir, Mack!" We knew not to argue - we were truly in the presence of a great man. It changed the way we looked at him. As if in awe combined with thankfulness and pride - I guess you could say honorable admiration. We exited the restaurant and he pulled up a rocker on the porch. We each sat on a bench, and while we all already knew the order, Brock made certain to sit close to our new mentor.

"I like this Mr. MacArthur," said Brock. "Sitting out here talking with you is nice."

"Well this is what us old timers would call 'Snap Chat,'" he said with a smirk and a snap of his fingers.

"And once your friend Cole stops laughing I'll give you some clues. See, if you take the modern Powersite Dam away that made this here lake, imagine this country just flowing with clear streams. Every good treasure hunter worth his salt would ask where the original dies are for the coins. Consider the stories of the Spanish Gold cave near Reeds Spring, the Marvel Cave, Bread Tray Mountain. Then think about what a General would do if Indians were chasing you downstream. You'd leave everything in an old mine behind and save your men, weapons, and food, wouldn't you? Then ask yourself if James thought the same way. He would have thought everyone would look downstream. But why wouldn't they have gone north, up the James River toward Galena, which was originally called Jamestown. I believe all these stories are connected, and that the original cave is hidden somewhere in the middle of all the locations listed. If you take a map and draw lines from the origin of each story, they will make an X - and we all know where you find the treasure on any map is always at the cross. Which will put you near Aunts Creek on the James arm of Table Rock."

The hair stood up on our arms. We couldn't believe he was sharing this with us. How did we get here, meet him - is this what you call luck? We were biking all over the hillside and just when we thought all was lost, we get a nugget of wisdom that changes our choices for the rest of the day, weekend, or maybe our lives. Thoughts were racing through our heads.

He began to stretch and said, "it's tough getting old. I'm headed north, and I imagine we're going the same way. So let's throw your bikes in the back of that white truck over there, and I'll get you closer to where you're going a little quicker. That way you'll have more time for treasure hunting."

He smiled as we looked over and saw a huge white horse of a machine with custom black wheels and the red words on the side that said 'Syclone'! I smiled as I'd heard about and seen this truck in Aurora at the GMC dealer.

"That bad boy is a GMC with a supercharged V6 pushing 455 horsepower, 425-foot pounds of torque and an 8 speed transmission that'll do 0-60 in 4.5 seconds."

"Well, first off," answered Mack, "she's a girl." He stood there helping us load as if protecting her. "And she's a good girl at that."

He carefully adjusted the bikes so they would ride sturdy, closed the tailgate and bed cover, and nodded appreciation as Brock held his door open for him. We climbed in and never said a word as we took in all her beauty. I'm sure it's not normal for man to love machines so much. He pushed the button that started an inspiring roar that sent vibrations deep into our souls. He pulled a white felt cowboy hat off the dash and pulled it down on his forehead, looked over at us and said, "Buckle up buttercups, let's arrive alive! Where am I taking you?"

Gage pointed north. "It's close to Aunt's Creek cove," he said, trying to talk over the rhythmic rumble of their ride. He looked over with excitement and said, "we'll go to Maya's lake house and figure out a way to get her Dad to fly us over the area so we can look for more clues."

"Fly?" Brock and Cole replied, still smiling from ear to ear.

"You'll see!" I said as the truck slowly rolled out onto our now lucky Highway 13 Wilderness Road. He looked over us and said, "if you're ready we'll make like buffalo and stampede this ole' game trail!"

I'm not sure what he was really thinking but I knew what to say, "Cole, put your phone down, and, Mr. Mack...Light 'em up!"

The whole truck drifted sideways, and the sound was invigorating - but the pressure felt like we were being shoved deep into the seats as we shot forward like a rocket. It was suddenly easy to remember our breakfast as it was once again back in our throats. He eased off the pedal and we straightened out and knew this ride would be over way too soon. It's like we had left our brains back at the take off because all we could say was, "Dude, that was Bad!"

Mack was even smiling, with his answer, "No that was Good, Dudes!"

Who would have thought an old man could be so cool? I directed us to the turn-off and we unloaded so we could ride in - it might be hard to explain Mack, the truck, and still keep Brock's secret.

CHAPTER FIVE

Provision Mapping

As we stood with our bikes, we wanted to pinch ourselves to make sure we were not dreaming. This was a super cool morning. How could it get better?

"Now you boys be careful and don't ever stop looking for treasure - with a goal of using it to take care of others."

He took out a card and a pen then wrote something down. He reached out to shake Brock's hand, holding the card together between them. He pulled him closer and explained,

"if you ever need a friend to talk with, please give me a call."

Then pulled him into his chest wrapping his arm around him for a big long hug.

"Thank you, Mr. MacArthur, you can...um..."

He quickly interrupted Brock, looked down at his head and corrected him saying, "son, please call me Mack."

We all had grateful grins on our faces as we got on our bicycles like Civil War soldiers mounting their horses and heading off to battle. Brock turned and said, "Mack if we find it, we'll let you know."

He smiled and said, "son, don't say 'If,' but boldly speak 'When' and I'm sure I'll hear about it when you do!"

We rode down the hill to Maya's, and at the corner I stopped them for a "little talk" that had been weighing heavy on my mind.

"Ok guys, here's the deal. That man reminded me the importance of honesty. So, while I respect our goal and am willing to keep your secret, I will not lie to Maya or her family. Here's the deal: don't say anything you need me to agree with that's not the truth. That doesn't mean you have to tell everything you know, but don't be dishonest or misleading. Got it?"

"Yea, but how are we going to get him to take us flying?"

"We can try to get him to take us flying because we really want to go for the super cool experience, and you can look around for clues all you want and we can discuss them later, just don't lie anymore, okay?"

"Alright!"

"Are you sure?"

"Yes, we got it."

"Then what do we say as to why are we just rolling in on our bicycles?"

"Can we just tell them we were at Clearwater Cover Camp and came over to see her?" "That wouldn't be a lie, it just wouldn't be telling the whole truth."

"And how did we get our bikes there?"

"We hauled them. We sure didn't ride them all the way to Kimberling City, now did we?"

"How about this, said Cole. "If they ask questions, we'll change the subject by answering with more questions they don't want to answer. My Mom does it all the time to my Dad, so I've seen it work."

The look on Maya's face was epic when we rolled down the sidewalk to the boat dock. But even more so was the look on Cole's face when he saw the Cygnet.

"What in the world is that?"

"It's an amphibious, flex wing microlight. Or in other words, a motor-propelled hang glider on pontoons with re-tractable wheels."

"Coool! Does it fly?"

"Well, Cole, that wing isn't there as boat shade." It's hard to distinguish if his look back at me was from excitement or elated confusion to understand a little bullish banter.

As Maya jogged to the dock ramp, I knew the next words coming out of her mouth" "What in the world?! Did you ride your bikes all the way here to see me?"

"Yes," I said with a smile.

Brock was almost laughing at me and with a quiet snark I could hear him say, "the truth will set you free!"

"Well actually," I said, "we rode here from Clearwater Cove. We had a project there this morning and brought our bikes so we could ride over here."

Maya scowled her forehead and stated, "I've been texting you all morning."

"Uh, my battery is dead. Do you have a plug I can use?

"Sure, it's in the boat."

Before I turned around my brothers from another mother had kicked off their shoes, peeled off their shirts and were bounding toward super splashville. "Ya-hooo" echoed across the cove. It was a relief to see Brock enjoying himself again. And hopefully it would distract from the looming questions I didn't want to answer. It didn't take long from the cannonball launch off the dock to find they had swum around and were gazing - or should I say drooling - at the Cygnet flying machine.

"Think we could convince your Dad to take them flying?"

"You know he would enjoy taking them almost as much as they will enjoy going."

"Enjoy? might be putting it lightly!"

"I was about take to the jet ski for a spin, want to go with me?"

"Sure, but what about them?"

"Can they ride?"

"I think so, but we better give some safety instructions about how not to run over us. Can we go to Aunt's Creek Cove?"

"Sure, it's close."

"Here put these on dudes, as I threw life jackets to them."

"Why? We can swim."

"Yes, but can you beat me or Maya on one of these?"

As air released from the jet ski ramps, they lowered into the water and were ready to slide backwards off the dock.

"This is paradise," said Cole. "What in the world does your Dad do for a living?"

"He's a business consultant." Maya paused with thought of how best to describe or explain to answer the next question.

"What is that?"

"He invests in businesses, then helps them with profit improvements and continued growth."

"Listen close, my friends," said Gage. "No fancy flip tricks trying to splash anyone. Green and gregarious jet ski riders keep the emergency rooms full around here. Be smart and careful - we can take risks with treasure hunting, but not with someone else's property."

"Ok, dad, we got it!" snarled Cole.

"Treasure hunting?" said Maya with a raised eyebrow. "Are you guys down here searching for that treasure we heard about in Mr. Stewart's class?"

Brock looked at Gage. Cole looked at Brock. I looked at both of them. Then they looked back to Maya and at the same time. "No!"

My reply was, "maybe. Why?"

That's when they both looked me and said, "GAGE!"

"First off, I didn't tell her, she guessed - she's very smart you know. Second, I told you I would not lie to her."

"So, we are hunting treasure. That's cool!"

"We? She's getting part of your share, Gage."

As the skis roared to life, the ducks shuffled quickly away as we left the dock and idled out toward the "No Wake" buoy. Everybody wanted to go fast, but we knew the waves would rock the boats causing the parents to shake their clenched fist at us while yelling something about kids and respect. I loved the sound of the waves splashing against the ski. Brock looked at me, then Maya, and shook his head. He clearly did not understand this girl-crazy thing that made me want to be so good. Once we reached the idle buoy a simple squeeze of the throttle and the ski nose reared its head out of the water and the race was on. Somehow Maya had once again positioned herself in front. Maybe it's her fun competitive spirit I admire so much, but she brings the best out in me - that's for sure. We all ran wide open, with the wind in our face and the sun on our backs. It was a great day on the lake! Just then we saw Maya go airborne - she'd hit a rogue wave which should have made us slow down but there was no way she was giving up first place. We bobbed the waves, weaving and working our way up the main arm to Aunts Creek then headed for the back of the cove. The green trees lined the rocky shoreline encasing bluish green water that had turned so smooth it was like glass. Slowing we stopped in the middle like circling the wagons. Shutting off the motors, the waves quickly settled and we noticed how quiet everyone and everything had become in comparison to the ride.

"What are we looking for, Brock?" asked Maya.

"Well....not really sure yet."

He shared the story of Mack, the 4 locations, and that this was the center of it all.

"It's just a hunch. We are exploring for clues, but I don't know what to do now as I don't see anything here."

You could see the pressure on his face and hear the frustration in his voice.

"I get that you want to find it, but don't let it get you down," said Maya.

He looked at us and we gave him a nod. "Tell her, I said."

He began to explain about his mother, her need for a healed heart, and made her promise not to tell anyone. Maya's eyes teared up. This girl might be competitive but her heart melts for huggable puppies and humble people. He explained what we had learned and after a few more minutes she said, "It's cool you've so much information already. I've got an idea. We can't see anything from down here. Let's go back and I'll get my Dad to take you up in the Cygnet and you can look for clues among the clouds."

"That's awesome!"

I knew what was coming next, so I started my ski and got turned around so I could beat her out of the cove. She knew what I was doing as I was grinning ear to ear. She started her engine and the quiet cove suddenly came alive.

Upon return to the dock we ramped the skis and the boys jumped in and swam over to and around to the Cygnet. Treading water, their inquisitive eyes gazing from one end to the other over the flying contraption. The two red pontoons held it out of the water with rear wheels on the side that attached to a lever and folded up out of the way with one wheel in the front making it possible to make it land or take off on water or dry land. Between the pontoons was a cross bar carriage that supported what looked like part of a small snowmobile - it had two small seats right in the middle, the one in back sat a few inches higher than the front and was right in front of a little motor attached to a big propeller. The seat in front had kind of a cockpit with a very small windshield and gauges. Above the whole thing was attached to a giant red, black and white hang glider-style wing with a triangle steering bar that hung down in front.

Nate had seen the boy's heads bobbing like ducks around his flying toy and was coming down to see Gage and check on everything. As soon as they saw him coming across the ramp they swam backwards and around to the dock ladder.

"You boys are friends of Gage?" he asked.

"Yes, Sir!"

"Nate," he said, as he extended his hand out to greet them. They weren't sure how to ask, but they had to know what it would feel like. Just as Brock tried to mumble a question, Nate interrupted them with, "so, which one of you is going first?"

Cole quickly replied, "Brock! You go right ahead. There is no way you're getting me in that crazy thing, if we were meant to fly like that we'd been born with wings."

Nate smiled and began to give instructions to Brock as he was already standing next to him. He steadied the machine with a rope while Brock eased onto the carriage into the back seat which sat right in front of the engine. As he pulled the 5-point belt buckle over his shoulders you could see the look on his face bounce from fear to fantasy as he put his helmet on. Once Nate was in position, he snapped his helmet, turned on the microphone, and all of sudden Brock heard the words, "testing, testing."

"Can you hear me, Brock?"

"Yes, sir!"

He started the engine, and the propeller began spraying a mist behind them. Slowly pulling away from the dock and headed out to the mouth of the cove, Nate pulled the wing bar towards him and began to move it around while looking up. He pointed up and toward the center of the wing where it met the carriage post.

The way Brock tells it, his adventure went something like this. And of course I believe him as Iv'e been there myself.

"You see that, Brock?" Asked Nate.

"What?"

"That bolt that connects the wing to our plane?"

"Uh, yes!"

"That's called the Jesus bolt, that's the only thing that keeps us from falling," he said with a sly grin.

He looked back to see that we were far enough away from the dock, then began to accelerate the engine. He said that he wasn't sure if he should look backwards forwards or down. Water was spraying from the sides of the pontoon and all he could see beneath his feet was the lake rushing by. Faster and faster they went. Describing how the pontoons seemed to start skipping on the surface. The noise from the roaring engine and the rushing water was incredible. Then, all of a sudden, he pushed the bar forward and the wing tilted up, the pontoons broke free from the water and they began to rise. But the startling part was that now the whole machine swayed around under the wing until they became balanced. He explained how everything got quiet as the water dropped below them and the motor noise disappeared behind . The wind in their faces, they climbed up toward the low hanging clouds and everything below became smaller and smaller. We laughed as he told us that he never knew his heart could race so fast while sitting down. Nate drew the wing in a move to the left, and the Cygnet stopped climbing and turned to the right. Every boat on the water was looking at them. It was the most amazing feeling of freedom. He had never flown on a commercial airplane, but in comparison he imagined this would be like stepping off of a school bus and getting on a motorcycle! They both provide similar transportation and can get you to the same destination, but one is way more fun and free than the other. They were high enough that he could see both arms of the lake and imagined when they were just two merging rivers. Nate keyed up the mic again in Brock's helmet and with a laugh said, "I can hear your breathing has finally slowed down - can you speak yet?"

All he could say was, "WOW! Amazing!"

Then he remembered why he was up there. "Can we go up the James arm to Jamestown?"

"To what?" said Nate.

"Oh, I mean Galena."

So, without a word he pushed the bar to the right and the big beautiful red bird they sat under elegantly flew to the left. They soared over the trees and flew north up the lake. You don't know where to look: up, down, left, right, forward, backward...the world beneath was like a beautiful painting. As they flew over the green trees of the ridge, the picturesque blue water would shine their shadow below. The lake narrowed and they could see a small town ahead.

"There's Galena, "Nate exclaimed as he pointed off to the left.

The lake had become a river and the ridges had become green fields. He turned and pulled the bar toward them and lowered them down to glide over one of the fields. As they dropped in altitude, they drifted effortlessly over the grass and soared over a herd of deer. The deer began to run as they glided over them like a historic pterodactyl that was about to scoop them up. They came to the edge and he pushed the bar forward, revved the motor, and they climbed again to turn back towards the river. As they circled and turned to go back, they dropped over the edge of a ridge. That's when they saw it. A cave in a tall rock bluff that seemed almost white in color. It was right over the river, surrounded by trees with no road anywhere in site.

"What is that?" Brock yelled.

"That is what we would call a 'cave,'" Nate responded with a snicker.

His mind was racing as he thought about what we'd learned. What if Mack was right and they travelled up the river by boat to the cave?

"You ever hear the story of the Yocum dollars," he asked.

"Yes," said Nate, as he curved back to the left.

"Do you know where the old Spanish treasure cave is?"

He pointed ahead. "It's just north of Reeds Spring, that way."

"And Marvel Cave - where is that?"

He pointed straight ahead. He curved the bird back south and said, "but we're going that direction back to the boat dock."

His mind was still racing as he looked in each direction of every story we had heard. He was distracted and lost in thought when he realized they were getting closer to the water and going very fast. You'd think he would be comfortable by now, but he hadn't given much thought to landing. It was very scary compared to the takeoff, as they were gliding in quickly and it seemed as if they were going to nose dive into the water. At the last minute, though, he pushed the bar forward and changed the whole pitch and speed; that carefully sat the back of the pontoons onto the water and glided the front down smoothly. As they slowed, he could see the dock ahead. We taxied over and everyone was smiling at him. "How could they see the hair standing up on my arms from so far away?" he wondered. He pulled off his helmet and carefully worked his way back onto the dock.

"Well?" I said, "how was it?"

"When I'm rich, which is going to be very soon, I'm going to become a pilot!"

Nate looked over and said, "you don't have to be rich to be a pilot!"

"Ok, how to you become one?"

"The same way you do anything in life. If you have a dream, write it down.

It's called Provision Mapping. Your dreams written down with details becomes your life's map. All great adventures require a map, provisions, and bold persistence to challenge the obstacles along the trail. So, dream big, always carry a map, plan your provisions, choose an experienced guide and reliable companions, be prepared to make your own trail, and remember dreams are better when achieved together!"

"Hold everything, who's got a pen and paper? Can you slowly run that by me one more time so I can write it down?"

"I'll do better than that, Brock." He reached into his pocket pulled out his wallet and removed a stack of cards. "Here, turn it over and what I just told you is printed on the back. Keep this and let me know when you're ready to take action and I'll guide you around the obstacles."

With a firm handshake and a sincere "thank you," Brock turned and waved us his direction.

"Let me tell you about what I saw." We headed for the other end of the dock and sat down to hang our feet in the water listening to Brock explain the excitement and views of flying in the Cygnet. Everyone's mind wandered and wondered as we stared into our reflections shining in the calm cove water. We couldn't see far beneath the surface, but our imaginations created hope if for no other reason but that we were all together. Two mallard ducks were floating and flirting near us, the bright colors of their plume glowed in the sunlight and the way that Drake seemed to be protecting the Hen was picture-perfect.

Brock moved his legs to create waves on the surface, looked up in thought and said, "I think Mack was right! It all makes perfect sense seeing it from above. If I was Yochum and I had the Spaniards' stash I would certainly have paddled up the James River away from the Indians and the old fort. And I saw a cave in a bluff right on the river above Jamestown."

"Ok, but how in the world can we get there to check it out?"

"I know, we'll call my brother Caleb."

"Well, I get how he could help as he's almost tall enough to see in the cave without climbing the bluff, but how would he help beyond that?" barked Cole?

"You guys may not know this because he doesn't like us to talk about him, but Caleb scored in the top 1% of the nation on special aptitude exams 5 years in a row. You wouldn't know it because he is so calm and cool, but Caleb is an Einstein! He's also my protector so if we're going to continue this adventure and face any danger, I know my Dad would trust Caleb to watch over us. He'll know what to do and how to help."

Maya's goldendoodle Gracie stopped staring at the ducks and looked at us as if to grin and nod that she agreed we were on the right path - or she was just happy to be part of our pack and close to the water. Either way, the love and loyalty of that gorgeous animal could teach us all how to be better friends! Brock was antsy and announced, "we need to get up and ready to roll!"

We weren't sure where, but he was ready. I was not near as excited as that meant leaving Maya behind. That's when I got a text from Caleb saying he could meet us with the canoes in Galena tomorrow morning - which gave me a great idea.

"Hey Maya, want to go floating and help us find the treasure tomorrow?"

Her smile was enough to melt my heart. I'm not sure what it is but she has it. Pure perfection!

"Slow down Brock, let's think about this for a sec. We spent last night by a leftover campfire. What makes you so sure we'll be as lucky tonight?"

"Well I'm far more worried about biking all the way to the James River than where we'll sleep."

"How about we try to plan for both, then."

"You slept where?" asked Maya with raised eyebrows.

In perfect fatherly fashion Nate strolled up. "Why don't you boys stay for dinner? Marci went to the farmers market yesterday and she's fixing fresh green beans, corn on the cob, fried gold potatoes - and she's got jerk chicken marinating that I'll grill on the barbie. You can spend the night on the dock, and I'll drive you to the river in the morning."

"Well, Brock, it looks as if you're outnumbered on this one. We both know Cole is going to vote for dinner here!"

And, as expected, Cole is nodding, "you know it's true!"

"But I have to ask, I didn't know chickens had personalities - so what made the one you're cooking such a jerk?"

Even Nate was laughing. "Now, that's exactly why we are eating him."

CHAPTER SIX

The Family Feast

"I just texted Caleb and made plans to meet him at the old Galena bridge with the canoes in the morning. So, until then, it's time for some more cannonballs off the end of the dock!"

"After me, Gage"...and as Maya jumped up we knew the race was on. All had good intentions to win but nobody ever outruns Brock. Kapushhh! went the sound of summer as the loud refreshing sprays went off like water fireworks in all directions. The ducks that had been casually swimming nearby in hopes of a crumb or two bugled their horns and beat the water with their wings as they escaped our water attack. Laughing makes swimming much easier, but everything came to an abrupt halt when we saw Maya's mother carrying a basket of goodies down the ramp to the stone garden & grill picnic area at the top of the dock ramp. Oh, don't get me wrong; we were all still smiling, but Marci carried a presence about her that was a good blend of fun with a little pinch of "let's get things done," so we knew it was time to help. The rock oasis was right next to the water, with huge flat stones laid end-to-end separating the bright green yard from the lake with a trail of steps leading back to the house. There was a huge picnic table in the middle with a grill full of flames at the end.

Brock was not use to this family picnic stuff, but you could tell he loved it. From the tablecloth-covered table with bright fresh flowers in the center glowing orange from the evening sun to the sweet smoke-filled air from the grill. Nate and I were grilling the jerked chicken and the sweet hot pepper marinade charred the skin to a crispy dark golden brown. When the last piece came off the grill, we were all waiting and our mouths were watering from the beautiful bounty that laid before us. Maya's grandparents had arrived and had brought a basket of jalapeno-cheddar corn muffins that were calling my name. Neither Cole nor Brock were sure what to do, but followed our lead as we all gathered around the table and held hands to offer grace-filled thanks for such wonderful food, family, and friends! Once everything had been passed and our plates were full, everyone got quiet (except for Cole - once he got ahold of the corn he ate it like a wild man who hadn't eaten in a while). He hadn't looked at his phone since the chicken hit the grill. As he moaned and chomped on the cob we could barely make out that he was asking what the red stuff was.

"It's sprinkled with a chili pepper lime aioli," said Marci with her proud motherly smile.

"I'm not sure I still know what that is, but it's delicious!" he said with a confused look of satisfied curiosity. "And the green beans, these don't taste anything like the school's."

"Well these aren't canned; they were blanched fresh then placed in an ice water bath to shock the chlorophyll so they would stay bright green, then I smothered them in grilled Vidalia onions and crispy peppered bacon with some of the grease mixed with some apple cider vinegar and sea salt."

All we got back was a nod, a smile and, "can I have some more please, Mrs. Marci?"

We all ate so much it was going to be hard to stand up. We noticed Brock eating, and, without saying a word, he would look at Nate and Grandpa, then back to Nate as if studying them with deep thoughts. Nate announced, "let's help the ladies carry this mess back up to the lake house then we can finish this evening with a big boat ride."

"Could this day get any better?" I thought as we all stood up to help.

The boat was big alright. I'd call it more of a fresh water yacht! We admired the couches and recliners that surrounded the captain's chair and peeked into the door that led into the nose. It had a huge bed, bathroom, and...yep, you guessed it, a kitchen sink.

"This is where you guys can sleep tonight," explained Maya.

"Uh, really? When you said 'sleep on the dock' I was hoping we didn't roll off the side but this thing is nicer than my own bedroom."

"Yeah, about last night's sleep question...you dodged when my dad showed up. I haven't forgotten that yet," she said with a grin. "You've got some stories to tell when this is all over."

We heard everyone board, then the big motor started and the deep rumble seemed to purr like a huge wild cat. Nate backed the big beast out of the slip and idled out to the buoys. Then he laid down the throttle and the rumble turned into a roar as she raised up and parted the water with ease. Once again everyone was quiet and smiling as the breeze blew our hair back and the setting sun gently kissed our cheeks. The boat cut through a big wave, and the spray shot out from the sides of the boat just as I gazed at Maya. The sun was right behind her head, so the water created a rainbow around her like a halo. She caught me and giggled, then looked away quickly which reminded me that I was staring at her in front of her whole family. I should have known better than to see if they noticed - they were all smiling at me. Lord have mercy! Since there is no hole to crawl in, should I just jump overboard now? All was soon forgotten as the sun grabbed everyone's attention. It lit up the layers of clouds with orange, red, and purple hues. It seemed to be trying to reach out and touch us as it glistened on the sparkling waters and followed our boat." We glided across the surface and then all too quickly the sun disappeared with a wink behind the gorgeous dark green Ozark mountain. Before we knew it, we were back at the dock and I realized I hadn't paid any attention to Brock and Cole. They were both so mesmerized by Captain Nate's nautical gauges they hadn't thought about me, either.

Everyone headed up to the cabin as Marci made sure we understood the 'stay safe and smart' rules. It was way early to be going to bed, but after the short night and long eventful day I wasn't going to argue. It was amazing how good the bed felt and the occasional wave would rock us like babies in a bassinet. That's when Brock broke his long silence. With a sad voice he said,

"Why can't I have a family like you guys? It's not fair. You both have dads and big families that do things together and have so much nice stuff."

"Don't speak for me," remarked Cole. "My Dad is dead drunk by dark so don't include me in your little woe-is-my-little-family fairy tale."

"Listen guys, no family is perfect, but what I've learned from Maya's family is that they are willing to give more than they take. It seems crazy but it's as simple as love and respect. Did you notice how the men are greatly respected and in turn they truly treat the ladies with honorable love? We can't choose our family, but our future is absolutely our choice. I love my father and mother but I also want a family like Maya's, so I plan to work hard and live an honorable life - to try my best to always have a thankful and positive attitude with a heart to love others...and maybe someday I'll gain the respect that the leaders of her family have."

"I like that, Gage! I never want to forget this day. I hope we are always friends and make sure we stay on the right track. But most of all I hope we find the treasure."

He paused. "Hear what I'm say'n? I don't know how to explain my crazy decisions, but sometimes I get a thought and feel pulled toward something, someone, or someplace...not knowing why or what the outcome will be. Then when the waves come, I second-guess myself, question my sanity, and worry about the outcome, until all of a sudden I'm caught in the middle of an incredible, indescribable adventure in my life...it's like someone or something is directing me toward good, but if I resist and choose to not move or stay where I am, then I end up sad and lonely. But if I stay strong and move forward with faith, it leads to unbelievable challenges that with time turns into amazing blessings! Know what I mean?"

"Uh, maybe, ok. Yeah, now please go to sleep, Brock."

It surprised me to be the first one to wake up, but they groaned and rolled over as I slid out the door. Maybe it's because I was hoping to catch a glimpse of the sunrise with

Maya. The lake was quiet, and the sky was getting brighter. The cool morning air seemed different than the city. Maybe it's because there's no concrete here to hold the day's heat. I turned as I heard the door close. It was Maya and she had a basket in her arms heading my way. I had to pinch myself to make sure I wasn't still dreaming.

"Good morning, Gage. My grandmother packed some cinnamon rolls and made you guys a thermos of hot cocoa. Here you are, handsome!"

She reached into the basket and handed me a blue ceramic mug. Then I noticed as she poured the steaming chocolate into the bottom it was full of marshmallows and they seemed to puff and float like clouds. Maybe I'm being sentimental about the small stuff, but man this gorgeous girl smells like a field of fresh spring flowers! I clearly got confused when her return smile turned upside down into a bit of a frown. She whispered lightly, "I can't go with you today. It's not because I don't want to, but out of respect for my family. I need to go to Church with them this morning."

"That's ok, Maya. After last night we all agreed your family is powerfully important to all of us. It gives us hope. Besides the boys get a little frustrated with me when you're around because I don't pay any attention to them."

We both chuckled and noticed the boat moving. We had tried to talk softly, but we both knew Brock wouldn't sleep much longer with treasure in his dreams – and Cole certainly smelled the cocoa. She sat out mugs for them, and they ate without saying a word. The rolls were very good, but getting to spend the morning with her is super sweet! By the time we finished our mugs and licked the icing off of our fingers Nate had come out to ask us if we were about ready. We felt like Secret Service when we piled into his big black suburban; Brock was glad to have an early start, and we were all filled with anticipation to see what our day had in store. Maya had brought us some food they packaged up from last night's amazing dinner, so we stuffed them in our back packs. That helped my heart as I waved goodbye to my friend so she could stay and help her family.

The big black beast wandered around the country roads toward our destination. It was at first quiet as our minds were full of yesterday's wonderful memories.

"Thank you very much for driving us, Nate," said Gage. "And for the dinner," piped Cole. "But mostly for the flight and sharing your family," Brock exclaimed pridefully.

The GPS was taking us down some strange roads as we cruised past Wolves stadium in Reeds Spring. and then we all noticed and pointed to the sign once we turned down Yocum Pond Road.

"Hey guys, this is what Mack told us! "The Yocum's would have traveled North up the River."

"Well, we're not near the James River yet, Brock."

"Look guys, Yocum Cemetery...Nate, can we please pull in and look for a sec?"

"Just a sec - I've got to get back and take my family to Church."

He slowed quickly and pulled over. The rest of us finally noticed the old man standing near the back looking at a tombstone.

"This is a bit strange, Brock. What do you expect to find here?"

"I won't know until I ask him."

"Who?"

"The old man. He looks sad like he misses someone, and he reminds me of Mack. So if nothing else maybe a respectable hello and a smile will make him feel better."

We watched in awe how Brock walked so casually over to the stranger with a soft concern for his well-being. Amazing how he was becoming aware of others through his own life struggles. We stood toward the front and watched awhile. We could see they were talking, and the old man smiled bigger as time went on as he pointed to different graves. Brock was right, it didn't matter that he didn't know us, what the old man needed most was someone to care enough to listen. Nate patiently watched with admiration and then finally whistled and motioned it was time to go. Brock gave the old man a good long handshake and then seemed to almost skip back toward us. We all got back in the Secret Service rig and headed back down the road.

"What are you grinning about Brock? What was that all about?"

"Well my friends," he slowly started. "My newly-found way of learning from my elders just paid off with another great clue."

"Oh, do tell, you rascal you," said Cole.

I thought Nate was going to drive into the ditch due to laughing at - or should I say "with" - us.

"He told me about some relatives that would tell stories about the old Yocum homestead. It's a few miles above Galena on the James. He said they changed the name to Camp

Blackstone. Back in the early 1800's you could rent a cabin and boat for twenty one bucks a week."

"Aaaand, how is that a clue, Mr. Smarty Pants?"

"Glad you asked! There is a cave located in white rock bluff just across the river. So imagine if that cave was across from an old Yocum homestead, and it was the same one I saw from the Cygnet. Wouldn't that be a great place to look for treasure?"

We all just nodded and dreamed as Nate pulled past the old bridge and announced we were almost there. We travelled under a big train tunnel, then saw Caleb's Jeep ahead at the old Galena Bridge loaded with three boats on the roof. As we unloaded the bikes and mounted them on the Jeep hitch rack, we all greeted then turned to thank Nate. They once again started talking about all his stuff, he looked at us with a stern face and said, "listen up friends, you are good boys and I'm proud to know you. But you must be happy with what you have. See, I could just as easily be jealous of you. You're free to go on adventures and experience life as young men. When you get older and you have all this stuff, you'll soon realize you spend all your time taking care of the stuff instead of each other. All that stuff can rust and fade away, but the memories and friendship you boys are making this weekend will never go away...nobody can take them from you. You have already put yourself on the right track to achieving your dreams!"

"Wait, I got it!" exclaimed Gage. "My dreams written down becomes my life's map. All great adventures require a map, provisions, and bold persistence to challenge the obstacles along the trail. Dream big, always have my map, plan my provisions, choose an experienced guide and reliable companions, be prepared to make your own trail, and remember dreams are better when achieved together."

"Coool!"

"Jinx, you owe me a Soda."

"What?"

"I'm lost."

"So am I."

"Then get out your map."

"Stop!"

"Ok boys,: said Nate, laughing with us. "Have a good day and take care of each other!"

"Bye, Nate! Thanks again, sir!"

CHAPTER SEVEN

River Runs with Honey

"Suup, Caleb? Thanks for bringing us the boats."

"Ok guys, here we are, but what's the plan?"

"Well, we don't really know. We need to find old Camp Blackstone, which is the old Camp Yocum...but we really have no idea where it is aside from upstream from Jamestown on the River."

"Well, now I'm certainly confused because we're on the James River at Galena."

"Same thing!"

"We'll explain on the way."

Caleb stretched and yawned as if he was about to start or finish something. He was always thinking.

"I've got some friends at school that have a family farm upstream. I texted her earlier to see how - or if - they could help us get our boats shuttled upstream so my Jeep will be here when we take out. Honey said she would meet us here, then they would take us to show where their farm is and to say hello. It's on the way. And here she comes. So, if you will all get in then we can get this party started."

It was like a scene from an Eagles song. This bronze skinned blonde pulls up wearing a bent straw cowboy hat driving an old blue step side farm truck with wood panel rails.

"Suup, Caleb! Hello, boys." She nodded and grinned at our stares.

"Hi, Honey."

We all looked at her, then at Caleb, then at each other and back at her. Before we uttered a word she said, "it's my nickname...got it cause I'm so sweet. You fellas ready to roll?"

"Yes, ma'am," Caleb answered.

And with that she pulled past us, and yanking on the big steering wheel she turned that truck around us so we could follow her down to the Conservation access. Clearly she had Caleb's attention as his head turned right along with her truck. We loaded our boats into the back of her farm truck and climbed in. We were smashed together and holding on for dear life as she climbed the winding hills toward their family farm. That's when we saw it. Just like before we all gasped when we looked at the road sign and it stated just as clear as day "Yocum Drive."

"Are you kidding me?"

"This is unbelievable!"

"How in the world?"

We all had a statement to the irony of chasing treasure clues across the Ozarks, only to end up finding this place without rhyme or reason. It couldn't be this easy could it? It's almost as if we are ending up at the right place at the right time without any idea where we are or where we are going. It's like our trail was laid out for us - we just had to take the risk of moving forward. And so, we went forward down the Yocum Drive almost to the end when we turned into a gravel drive. We pulled up to a little cabin by a pond full of ducks on top of a big hillside orchard and garden. There was a creek that started near some big rocks behind the cabin, then meandered through the pond and down right through the middle of the garden. As we parked and got out, Honey introduced us to her brother Willy. As we followed them down the hill, they showed us row after row of root vegetables topped with beautiful bright green leaves with hints of orange red and white roots peeking up from the rich soil. There were all variety of lettuces, and berry patches full of cascading colors of ripe fruits. There were apple, pear and peach trees.

"Here, taste this!"

Willy pinched off a gooseberry and handed them to us. Cole was the first to try his. We watched his eyes squint shut as he bit into the bitter juice. He was all puckered up and looked like he was about to kiss his grandma. We all started laughing, which caused the chickens to scatter. As we walked among the bounty of food, the farm dogs followed us as if we were their long-lost friends. Brock began to tell them his story.

"Hey now, be careful not to give away too much of our story! Our cut keeps getting smaller."

Honey looked at us with one eyebrow lifted.

"We don't need a cut! We have all the provisions we need right here to survive happy and healthy – a garden, chickens, deer, family, friends, and all the fresh water we'll ever need right in our back yard. What else could we want?"

"Better yet, when the world starts to struggle and fight each other for what to eat, do you think you'll be able to live better in the city on silver or right here without any?"

"Well said, Willy. I see your point, and it's valid but I wouldn't trade much for the adventure we've had this weekend. You see, if we hadn't taken the risk to move forward we wouldn't be here to see you and this beautiful farm."

"Tell me about this adventure Brock."

He began to explain that we were looking for the Camp Yocum. As he described what we knew and how we got here,

Willy stopped in his tracks and pointed to the bluff in the distance.

"See that?" he said as he pointed over the field toward a huge cliff.

"Yea, why?"

"That's White Rock Bluff. You're standing right next to the old Camp. There are four old cabins on the shoreline right across from the middle of that bluff. And yes, there is a cave way up there."

"Can we go?"

"Well again, yes. But it's across and up the river and so we'll take you upstream to put in. Then, when you float back down a couple of miles and you see the old cabins, you'll know you're there. Well, most of them. One was recently vandalized by some disrespectful drunk floaters. People forget they are in playing in people's backyards. Anyway, you won't be able to get into the cave without some ropes. I've got some in the barn you can put in Honey's backpack and take with you. And before you do anything, you must remember to get permission. Both sides of the river are on private property. The river is navigable so you're free to use it, but anything you access above the high-water mark would be trespassing."

"Well, what are we waiting for?"

"Let the adventure begin!"

We headed back up the hill to Honey's truck with the dogs in tow.

"We'll have to put Sparky on a chain or he'll follow us all the way."

We all piled back in. Honey slid in behind the wheel, looked over at Caleb, then pulled it into gear. She gave him a wink and we headed up the drive and back up the road. The road was narrow and curvy, so all of us were glad to get out when Honey pulled up to the river access – well, all of us but Caleb. I think he would have stayed in that truck with Honey if given the chance.

"I'll see you boys at the bluff after I get my morning chores done," she exclaimed as she drove away while leaning out the window.

We didn't give it much thought. We were getting our gear in the boats.

"Don't argue about the boats," said Caleb. "You can take turns paddling each one. To start, Cole you get in the front of the Mohawk with me. Brock, you take the Bell Wildfire and Gage, you can float the kayak."

Cole didn't argue because the Mohawk was a big tandem with custom seatbacks, so it was going to be a comfortable and safe ride. The Bell was made of very light Kevlar and had a wilderness hull so there was an arched keel and the side corners were very rounded. Dad says they call that the reserve triangle. All I know is it feels wiggly in the hips until it hits rapids then it actually feels more stable than the big flat bottom canoes. It's so thin that if the sun hits it just right you can see light through the sides. I do like the kayak.

You sit low down inside so it feels like you're part of the water as it glides effortlessly across surface.

"Be careful with these boats guys. They are all from our late Uncle Kevin's. He was my dad's floating partner. They provide my dad with wonderful memories, so treat them with respect."

"Look, Brock - this hull design will have you switching your paddle back and forth all day if you don't learn the J stroke."

"Uh, J stroke?" Brock replied.

"Yes, said Caleb. "Like this: halfway through your stroke turn your top hand so that your thumb points to the water. This makes the blade make a J as it comes out and that corrects the forward stroke with a small side correction that brings the nose back into a straight glide."

"Wow! That really works."

"Great! You've got it."

The small splash of the paddles hitting the water was like a cymbal to the backdrop of birds that whistled from the treetops that surrounded us. We took everything in: the old logs laying near the bank hosted a row of turtles that were drying their backs in the sun. They watched us with great suspicion, and if we got a little too close they would slide into the water and dive for safety. Just then, a big Blue Heron speared a perch right from the shore with its long sharp bill and swallowed it whole. And just as we watched the bulge of its breakfast slide in a huge lump down its throat, it let out a load squawk. It stretched out it's huge expansion of wings and flew downstream staying just a few feet right above the water. There wasn't much to talk about now. Nature had our undivided attention, from the bright pinkish blossoms of rose mallow to the hummingbirds that hovered over the orange trumpet vine flowers cascading down the banks. It was the first time we were glad to see Cole taking pictures with his smart phone. This was a day to remember, wrapped in layers of green from the rich bushes of summer leaves that flickered in the breeze atop the brown weave of tree roots that seemed to hold the bank in its place.

"So, Brock, I know you really enjoyed the big fancy boat ride the other night. But you have to admit: the simplicity of paddling down a river, with no need for fuel, no noise from an engine, and certainly no reason to race. Isn't this in a way just as rich?"

"Well," said Brock, "that analogy works when comparing boats and the experience. But even all the beauty of nature can't come close to the joy I saw in the love of that big family.

"Yes, Brock, we know, you still feel everyone's better than you because you don't have a dad."

Cole looked over at us. "Well, you know my opinion. I have a big family full of love. It's just that sometimes my dad drinks so much it makes me think he hates something about himself or us. So until you've experienced that pain you can't begin to understand how we long for the love we saw last night. All the ads on television show people having fun while drinking, but the reality is much different for many. For my dad he is a good man, but after a few too many it's like his spirit changes. It starts happy but all too soon the bad habit gets heavy. Must be why they call them spirits. I might not be able to change him, and there parts of him I love with all my heart, and there are times I see him struggle to do better...but the booze starts to take over and he or should I say we all suffer again, so I hope I never start getting drunk like that when I'm older.

Caleb calmly looked over and said, "That's correct. If you can't change your circumstance then change how you choose to see it."

"What do you mean?" asked Brock.

"It's really very simple."

"Well, everything is usually simple for you," said Gage.

"How about you run that by us in a way we can understand?"

"Ok. If you look for the good in something you'll find it. Look for the bad and you'll find that, too! Whether a parent, a friend, school or a job. What you look for you will find, what you find you will attract, and what you attract you will become. It's your choice so you actually define your own destiny!"

After that, the only thing Brock saw was his shadow reflecting in the river.

"So, what your saying is if I look for a father I will find him?"

"No, what I'm saying is that how you see the world, others, and your own circumstances is a choice you make with your heart. You can be filled with love and gratefulness or hate and jealousy, all of which are absolutely the making of your character. If you choose love you will receive love, but if you choose anger and hate toward someone or something, then that too will consume you. But it's always your personal choice! Whatever you choose can't be hidden because it will always be visible in your words and actions! Basically, your life is a cumulation of all the choices you make, a direct reflection of the books you read, the friends you keep, and the love in your heart that you're willing to give away without expecting anything in return."

It was very obvious we couldn't argue with the "mind master."

"Where do you come up with this stuff, Caleb?"

"Well, actually that came from your Coach, our dad. See, his family divorced and he searched for a way to change his destiny just as you are yours. He was obedient in searching for a Church family for us so we could have other elders and brothers surround us with love and forgiveness. He made a choice hoping he could save us from the mistakes and pains of his life so he prayed with and for us often. In fact, he has prayed for you and still does!"

Our conversation and the following long silence made the trip go by quickly. The next thing we know a curve in the river brought us to a huge gravel bar. To our surprise there was Honey on top of a bright yellow kayak paddling upstream toward us.

"There's your bluff, boys," she hollered. Better pull over here.

She pointed with her paddle to a long gravel bar between us that was bordered by a large bank with some old wooden cabins sitting right on the edge. The cabins had cedar tree posts holding up the porch, and the roof was solid green with moss. If this was truly the old Camp Yocum, then that means those little wooden bungalows have to be well over a hundred years old.

We pulled our boats up on the bar and all stood gazing across at the huge rock bluff that cast its shadow across the river. We were in awe! It stretched from left to right longer than a football field and was higher than our school gym. But this was all rock that looked as if it had fought many battles with the raging river and always came out the victor. And just as majestic was its crown of clouds that the sun had just slipped behind. The cloud was shining bright rays of sunlight from the top, so it in all truth looked like a crown right on top of a mountain. And right in the middle, between some giant treetops, we noticed a dark spot that clearly was the entrance to a cave. We quickly realized this magnificent rock would not give up its secrets so easily.

There was no way we were going up from the bottom - and if the only way was to rappel from the top then how were we going to get to it? More importantly how could anyone else have made it there to hide anything in it? Brock had a strange look on his face that was a mix of dazzled and disappointed - yet still determined. Caleb looked at them and announced that our little mystery is not going as easy as you'd hoped.

"We may have to make a new trail."

"Huh?"

"Now, we can risk life and limb trying to climb that striped monster or..."

He grabbed the big waterproof dry bag from his canoe and reached inside to pull out a big box. As he laid it on the bank and slowly opened it, we all stood with our mouths gaping open in shock as he unfolded a flying drone. It was the coolest thing since...well, it was very cool!

"Are you planning what I think you're planning?" said Brock like a kid in a candy store.

"Yes, stand back whipper-snappers, and let me show you how big bro gets 'r done!"

He grabbed the controls, pushed buttons, and all of a sudden it began to buzz like a giant bug and lifted off the ground. Before you could say anything, it was cruising effortlessly through the air around the bank, across the river, and then shot up the cliff like a hummingbird on steroids. Even Honey was impressed! We were all staring in amazement until it closed in on the opening. Then we noticed Caleb slow it down and turn around to block the sun. He began intensely watching the little screen on the controls, like herons watching for sunfish. We all gathered around him to gaze at the screen with hopes we could all be the first one to see some treasure - it didn't matter - just something old and cool would make it ok! The fantastic little flying machine was giving us a bird's eye view of the old cave opening, but it was dark and bare, nothing in sight.

"This is crazy Brock, think about it a sec. We're young. If we try to climb the bluff, we are risking our life, so how in the world do you think old man Yocum could have climbed this and hoisted heavy loads of silver up there? I think you're barking up the wrong tree."

"But that's just it, if it was easy everyone would have already done it."

"You're also forgetting the most important part, Brock."

"What's that, Caleb?"

"Well, if we get up there and we find anything it would belong to the property owner because we would be trespassing."

Brocks shoulders dropped with his head as he stared at the rocks and mumbled, "why does everything have to be so hard?"

We all hurt for him. I put my arm around his shoulders. I wasn't sure where it came from, but I shared my thoughts. "It makes since that we just go ask permission, yes? Seems like that shouldn't be so hard."

By now Caleb had caught on and was flying over the top of the bluff. It got much smaller as it flew high enough to show the area and there it was: a farmhouse in the distance. We had gotten so wrapped in ourselves we forgot Honey was there until she gave us a little "um hm" sound.

"You guys certainly are on an adventure! Want to go meet the farmer who owns the land?"

All of sudden Brock had a sparkle in his eyes again.

"Absolutely! Can we go right now?"

"Wait," said Cole. "Is there any way we can eat first?"

"COLE, you can eat on the way."

"Let's go!"

"But we just got this float started," said Caleb. "Here's an idea, I'll stay here and work these banks with my fly rod."

Honey chimed in, "I'll keep an eye on him. You guys go back to the farm and have Willy drive you over to get permission, then we'll meet you back here. Deal?"

Brock was already getting in the canoe to head downstream.

Caleb got a kick out of Honey wanting to keep an eye on him - actually we all did. Caleb is one cool cat!

CHAPTER EIGHT

Light in the Darkness

Even though Willy seemed to know where we were going, it still seemed strange to drive down the long gravel road to the old farmhouse. It looked like the kind of place you see on TV where a fella in overalls is sitting in a rocking chair on the porch with a shotgun in his lap and a hound dog at his feet. If Brock was worried, he didn't show it as he was the first one out of the truck, he didn't even make it to the steps when a tall thin man pushed open the screen door, to greet him.

"Howdy, young man. What can I do for ya?"

Brock extended his hand to offer his most polite introduction.

"Willy says you own the property all the way down to the James River."

"Yes, I do. Bought it many years ago and it's not for sale."

"Well, I don't have any money to buy it, but we're wondering if you would give us permission to climb the cliff and enter the cave."

He leaned back and scratched his chin.

"I'm impressed you had the character to come ask...which leads me to my question, why would you wanna go and do that?"

Brock told him his story, about his mother's heart and our search for the treasure.

He smiled and said, "hang on to your britches son." He leaned toward the door and hollered, "Daisie Mae? Bring me some paper and someth'n to write with."

We could hear some mumbling then the door screeched open and a sweet little lady stepped out to greet us. She had long silky white hair a blue flowery dress and an apron around her waist. She smelled like fresh-baked cookies.

"Thanks, Shugga," he commented with a snicker. "Here." He handed the paper and pen to Brock. "Write this down. This here paper is permission to be on Mr. Elijah's land on, let's see what is today? August 7th and if'n anything was to happ'n to me in anyway good or bad it ain't his fault. Now you and your friends sign it."

Brock looked up at him then began writing again while reading aloud slowly, "and any treasure we find we'll give Mr. Elijah 10%."

Elijah had a huge belly laugh that finished with a wheezing sound that had all of us laughing.

"I hate to bust your bubble son, but you got that whole treasure story wrong. The Yocum's got their silver by trad'n peach brandy to the Delaware Indians, who had gotten the silver dollars as displacement payment from the US government. And I can guarantee you no homesteaders would've hid their treasure in a cave, they would have kept it right under foot in their cabin floors. The only people that would have been in that cave were the Indians, and the only living thing that's been there since are some wild critters of one kind or another. So here, I'll sign it but it's cry'n shame we have to."

"What do you mean sir, why is it a shame?"

Well son, we used to be able to shake a man's hand and give him your word. But because of them fancy city lawyers and politicians always changing everything we have to sign stuff now. I think your word is good, but the doctors say I'm dying and I'd give anything if something could save me. But my biggest worry is mak'n sure nothing happens to this place so Daisie can live out her days in peace."

Brock grabbed his phone and took a picture of the paper, and promised that whatever he discovered that he would share. We spoke our thanks and piled back in the truck and headed back to the farm.

As we paddled hard against the current to make it back upstream, we saw Caleb teaching Honey to fly fish. He was standing right beside her with his arm around her shoulders and his hand on top of hers. Together they swish the rod through the air pausing at each interval until the line floated and curled over their heads in a loop that looked like a brush painting a picture. It was truly moving art. The last pause forward gently laid the line down on the water. And it wasn't long until they jerked it back up in the air. Caleb yelled so loud I think they heard him back at the farm. We pulled our boats onto the gravel bar and just turned to watch when we saw the monster break the surface.

"AAAaaaarrrrggghhhh!!! Is that a shark?"

Honey was backing up to get on the bank, and very willingly handed the rod to Caleb.

"Oh my, what the...get me out here! Cole is laughing at all of us."

"That's not a shark, you snagged a spoonbill paddlefish. My dad caught one last summer down by Cape Fair. It probably swam upstream from Table Rock in high water and has been stuck in this big pool."

Brock didn't seem to care at all. Even with the excitement of Caleb's fight with the prehistoric creature all he could do was stare at the bluff.

"You guys are going to be all day trying to get that monster landed," he complained.

We were so enthralled with the battle of man and beast that nobody noticed Brock had paddled across the river, and, with the rope strung over his shoulder, was looking for a place to start climbing. Caleb had hung on as long as possible without breaking the line. We didn't want or need the fish, but we certainly didn't want to leave a hook in its back. So, once he got it close enough to the shore, Cole ran out and grabbed its long round paddle nose and drug it closer so he could remove the lure. We gazed in awe at the freshwater beast when I noticed something moving on the cliff.

"Hey...look...Brock is halfway up the cliff!"

Cole quickly grabbed the tail and drug the fish back into the deeps to let it go so it could grow some more. And, almost as quickly, jumped in and swam across to river to try and help Brock. By the time we all got to the base of the cliff Brock was standing near the entrance of the cave wrapping the rope around the base of tree, and then to a rock sticking out of the bluff. He threw the rope down to us and yelled, "Tie my backpack with flashlight to the end so I can hoist it up after you get up here."

"Well, I'm not letting him have all the fun," said Cole as he put on the backpack and started up the rope. About half-way up his excitement faded and we all realized his love for food was proving to be more beneficial for RBI's than belaying up bluffs! I was next, and I must say that I could do without this part of our little adventure. Not that I was afraid, but that I had my own plans for a future that hopefully involved a little less risk and a lot more Maya! Once at the top we all stood and couldn't decide if we should look inside the dark mysterious cavern or enjoy the view of the hues of colors that abounded from the Ozark hills and valleys. That's when we noticed the dark cloud that was drifting toward us.

"Why does it seem that something is always chasing me," snapped Brock? "I know I'm supposed to be looking for the good, but it gets hard when there is always a storm behind you."

It was an eerie feeling to crawl back into the cavern, soon we could barely see light from the entrance. Brock had the only flashlight, so we had to stay close together. You could feel each of us jump when we heard that crack of thunder outside. It echoed deep and we could hear the rain and wind blow across the bluff. I was worried about Caleb. I thought about everything at once. What about the squirrels that were scampering through the trees, what about the big blue heron? Where does he go to hide? And the deer that hide behind the wooded brush, what do they do when it storms? Do they worry? Do they have fear? It was a short quick storm with very little rain. As the winds died down and the entrance began to light up again, we crawled back to the entrance to check on everyone. Caleb had pulled the canoe up the edge of the bluff, he and Honey had turned it upside down and were sitting underneath it for cover.

"Everybody ok?" I yelled from the cave above.

"Yea, we're cool! Find anything?" Caleb yelled back.

Just then, as I turned around, the sun cracked through the clouds. As it shined through the entrance you could see the outline of what seemed to be a cross pointing to a rock on the wall several feet back from the entrance. As we inspected it further, we noticed it was a rock that had been shoved into an opening. "Let's see if it goes anywhere," said Cole. But as we tugged and pulled it seemed to be wedged in so hard that we couldn't budge it. "Here, let me try." I had grabbed my dad's Gerber scuba knife that was hanging on my waistband. One edge was sharp, one serrated and the end was like a big screwdriver. We wedged and wiggled the blade around the rock until it loosened up then we slowly slid it forward.

"Brock, shine your light here, quick!"

We peered into the shelf and there was a very old wooden box shoved back in a dry rock shelf. We couldn't breathe. Our hearts were pounding so loud it felt like our hearts would explode out of our chests. Brock grabbed my arm, I grabbed Cole. We were mesmerized with wonder as to what was inside. Together we each reached in to try and pull the box toward us. As we brushed away the debris we found a perfect arrowhead. If it wasn't for the box that would have been enough right there to make this adventure a success! But there was, in fact, a box in front of us, so we brought it forward and sat it down on the rock floor at our feet. As we looked at it and back at each other we all had the same expression of shock and smile. Then Brock let out a whoop and holler that let everyone in the valley know we had very good news!

"We can't open it here, we have to get it down the cliff first."

"Why?! No! What are we waiting for, Christmas? We didn't come this far to wait anymore."

"If we open it here we could lose all the silver on the way down."

We all sat in silence again wondering what to do. Well - almost silence...we could hear Honey and Caleb yelling at us from below.

"What is it! Come on guys, Talk to us!"

"Ok," said Brock. "Go pull up the rope."

So, we wrapped the rope around the whole box many times creating a protective barrier so that the rocks would not damage the box as we lowered it. We announced to Caleb that under no circumstances should they try and open the box before we are all down safe. He agreed and said he had been praying for us the whole time. I'm not sure that comforted Brock, but he slowly began to give the old box the descent from its old home above down to my brother. Cole went first, then Brock. I pulled the rope up, ran it around the tree and lowered both ends back down.

"Hold on to both ends very tight please. If you let one end go, I'll fall."

"What are you doing, Gage?"

"We can't leave this rope here. Others will try to climb this and get hurt."

I think we both heard our mother's voice in our heads ("Be careful") had been repeated by her more times than any other word ever! They tied each end around their waist as I worked my way down the wall. Once at the bottom it was obvious Brock should never have tried to climb this alone, and there was no way now that anyone was going back up. It was an emotional thing to watch the rope end go around the tree and fall down to us coiling up at our feet - near our box full of treasure. Add to that the emotion of Caleb grabbing me with his arms for a long brotherly bear hug, and it's easy to understand why we all had tears in our eyes.

"Now, listen," Caleb announced. "I've had plenty of time to think about this."

"The story you heard is that the treasure has riches beyond your wildest dreams and immortality against death. So, whatever is in this little wood box must be the most valuable thing in the whole world. I'm as excited as you guys to see what's inside, but I think we should get this box off this river and get the help of an adult."

"That's ridiculous," barked Brock. "I didn't need the help of anyone to get me this far."

"Well, as a matter of fact, you did. All of us helped in one way or another, and from what I remember you got plenty of help from the men you met along the way. Can we at least take it over to the gravel bar so I can get off of this ivy covered, snake-filled hill in case it storms again?"

We carefully laid the box in the canoe to keep it dry, and swam around the boat until we had it securely on dry ground. That's when we noticed that nobody had floated by in a while. The storm must have kept everybody back. But hearing voices around the bend made us worried about opening the box.

"Is that, nooo... can't be?"

CHAPTER NINE

Fight or Flight for Treasure Rights

"That's little loudmouth Chris from school! What's he doing here?"

"The librarian's son? Floating, it looks like."

"But don't you think that's a little suspicious that we just happen to see him here of all places. Cover up the box with this towel and our life jackets. Act like nothing is going on and we'll just let them float right on by."

"Hi guys, how's it going? Meet my momma's boyfriend Butch. Find the treasure yet?"

Our look at each other must have given us away.

"What are you talking about?" said Brock.

"Well, I was visiting my mom at the library and overheard you talking. It took me awhile to find you, but thanks to Cole's addiction to social media it was pretty easy. See, your smart phone puts a GPS address on every picture you take. A geek like me can easily find you if you're leaving a digital bread trail. Now here's your next problem. If that box came out of that bluff cave over there and I'm here with you when you open it, then I'm entitled to part of the treasure. So, let's open it up and see what I've won!"

Brock moved between him and the boat. "Chris, you little blood sucking leech! Better take a picture of him Cole, so somebody can GPS the last location of his feeble body floating downstream. If he doesn't get outta my face right now he's going to become paddlefish food."

"Easy, Brock," said Caleb. "I've got you."

With that Butch stepped forward and shoved Caleb. But in his cool cat fashion, he turned the other cheek and quickly explained, "Butch, since you aren't the smartest tool in the shed, I might remind you that we're all minors and pushing me was assault; so, if you don't take a step back we'll be calling the Sheriff. You'll have yourself some free accommodations at the Stone County jail."

"How can you be a minor? You're way over 6 feet tall."

"That's right, I am. So there's your second reason to back up! And Chris, Brock's right, you're not from around here and certainly was never invited, so we aren't in charge of you. But clearly we won't allow you to disrespect us anymore. You can stay here and party all you want, but we're going downstream. Your attitude tells me it would be much safer for you not to follow."

"Is that a threat?" screeched Chris with his ornery obnoxious voice.

"Take it how you want, just take it somewhere else as we're done talking with you."

We all pushed off and began to paddle away.

"Remember," said Caleb. "The only thing that makes a difference in a canoe is the hull and your padding skills. Dig deep with your strokes, remember what I taught you, and he'll never catch us."

We paddled hard and separated ourselves from him.

"The farm is close," said Honey. "We'll run up to the truck and roll right outta here. I'll drive you back to your jeep and you can get that treasure home where you'll be safe."

We felt better once we had a little distance between us, but we knew their intentions were no good so we were still very nervous.

Once we reached the river bank at the farm, we grabbed the end of the canoes in a row and ran uphill as fast as we could go. We threw them in the back of the truck and pulled the box up on our laps. Honey threw gravel as she popped the clutch and flew up the hill. We thought we were home free until we pulled the Jeep up to the bridge. All of a sudden lights and sirens came from both directions. The Sheriff had surrounded us, and told us to stay right where we are. We knew better than to run - we really had done nothing wrong. They sat us apart from each other along down the middle of the old Galena bridge with our treasure box right in front us, giving us stern instructions to wait while they were contacting all participating parties and our parents, since we were minors. We weren't sure what was going on but the pain of staring at that box was just about Brock's last straw. We should've known they would call mom and dad. So, as we waited, my mind became haunted by the lies I had told them and how disappointed my father might be with us. I almost didn't even care what was in the box, or thought it couldn't be worth losing the favor of our father! Once we saw Chris over by the Sheriff's car we began to piece it all together. The Sheriff pulled us aside one at a time and took each of our stories. Then we saw them talking with Mr. Elijah. He looked our way and gave us a nod and a smile. Then my heart stopped when I saw my dad. Lord, have mercy! Then we saw mom; clearly nothing or no one would keep her from getting to us. She ran over and wrapped her caring arms around my neck and as always, whispered gently in my ear, "I love you infinite!" She always made us feel safe. If I'm sure about anything in the world it's that my father loves her with all his heart and always will. Dad looked over to see we were ok, and listened as they talked to him. Just when we couldn't imagine it getting any crazier a van pulls up from the local news channel and a camera man starts filming everything. Our head dropped as dad and the Sheriff headed this way with the news camera in tow. Our dad looked at us with a stern face, "you boys ok?" "Yes, sir! "Then the Sheriff spoke, "Well, boys, your story checks out. Mr. Elijah showed us a signed paper that he gave you permission to be on his land and that you could keep anything you found. He's an honest man so you did well to gain his respect. However, this Chris kid over there obviously has no legal right to the treasure whatsoever and even worse has cost our county a lot of money with this false report against you. In fact, do you want to press charges for the assault by his friend? It seems your brother handled the situation like a man, and I'd be glad to cuff them if you want me to. Just say the word."

"No sir," said Caleb. "Hopefully they learned a lesson."

"I know we did!" said Gage.

"What lesson is that, son?"

"Never, ever lie to your father!"

"Yes, and remember, nothing you ever do can make me stop loving you!"

"Hi, Coach!"

"Yes, Brock, you know I love you too! But we've all got some things to talk about."

"Sir?" said Brock. "Can I please open this box now?"

"Sure. What are you waiting for?"

"Uh...that's not even funny!"

Brock almost jumped all the way to the box. We all gather around with the dad, the Sheriff, Mr. Elijah and Daisie Mae, Honey, and even the news lady with her camera guy. Chris stood in the distance and watched with jealousy as I pried the edge of the box open with my knife, and Brock pulled it up and lifted it to the side. There was another leather covered box inside, and on top an ornate metal cross that was so heavy we were certain it was silver or gold. We lifted it out and sat it on the concrete bridge. Carefully unwrapping the old leather casing, it was hard and kept its shape as it lifted off. We were very confused that this was obviously not gold or silver. "It's a book?" We dusted the surface lightly, and, as we all leaned close, we could see the word "Gutenberg."

All of sudden, dad exclaimed, "my God in Heaven! Don't touch a thing, boys. That's a Gutenberg Bible. The last know copy was purchased by the University of Austin in 1978 for 2.4 million dollars!"

Tears rolled down his cheeks and filled the dimples from his huge smile. We all stared at it with our mouths dropped so far open our jaws were sitting on our chests.

"So what it's worth today, Coach?" asked Brock.

"Hard to say. We'll have to get it appraised, but my guess is it's several million. How did you find it? I mean how did it get in the cave?"

"Must have been when the Indians killed DeSoto and the Spaniards fled with Alvarado. They must have left it behind and the Indians hid it because it looked valuable, but they clearly would not have been able to read it."

"Oh Dad, check out this arrowhead we found next to it."

"Cool, Gage, but I'm overwhelmed with this treasure. Do you know why it's worth so much? Gutenberg invented the printing press. Before it existed, scribes would painstakingly hand write every word of the Bible onto parchment, making sure to keep the lines straight, the words the same size, and if any of the scripture was altered it would cause their death. It would take so long and was so expensive that only priests would have them for reading to the parishioners. The printing press would eventually be the reason that all of us can a have a copy of our own to read in our homes. And if that wasn't enough, then consider that this is revered as the most artistic and beautiful version ever. You, my sons, have found the figurative Holy Grail of literature!"

"All that sounds really cool, but not sure how that is going to help my mother."

My mom looked at him with her warm motherly way. "Son, your faith guided you this far, so don't let it fade now. It's Sunday, and after all this excitement we all could use a little rest, so come home with us and we'll pray for wisdom and our purpose."

I never thought I would be so happy to share our adventure stories with my father, but he smiled ear to ear while he listened to our tales all the way home. Caleb and Mom followed us, and we all felt so relieved that there was no judgment for our mistakes. Not sure how we are going to sleep - or should I say when we are going to get up. My satin pillow case was most certainly calling my name.

CHAPTER TEN

Rich Advice

"Wake up, boys!"

My mother was gently kissing my cheek. What a way to greet the day. Brock moaned and rolled over as his mind and strength was exhausted.

"You were on the news last night. Some man called this morning, and is flying in to meet you because he wants to buy the book."

Brock sat straight up but his eyes were still half closed.

"How much?"

"We don't know yet. He's flying into Branson, and wants us to meet him at the College of the Ozarks."

"Can we sleep in the car on the way there?"

She laughed and agreed. "But first let's get some pancakes in your bellies."

"I'm up," said Cole as he wiggled out of his sleeping bag on the floor.

"Oh, I called your parents, Cole, so they now know where you are."

"Why are you guys not at work today?"

"Well, given all the excitement, we decided to take the day off. It's a good thing - your little adventure may pay off well. We - all the parents - are meeting today to help you handle the small stuff like bankers and lawyers."

The ride back to Branson was quiet, not because we didn't have a thousand questions, but that it didn't make sense to ask since we really had no answers.

We hadn't even made it through the Keeter Center doors when Brock's mom Kayla grabbed him and wouldn't let go. Cole's parents were behind her waiting as Cole ran up and grabbed them both. A student approached us from the Dobyn hostess station.

"I recognize you boys from the news! Please come with me. Mr. Consejo is waiting for you in the Basore Presidential Dining Room."

This was surreal, I thought. How did we go from a baseball game to the clubhouse and end up here?

We entered the restaurant and followed her to a private room. A dark handsome man stood up to greet us. Two men in black suits stood behind him with their arms crossed.

"Hello gentlemen, my name is Rico."

We each introduced ourselves and our parents.

"Sit please. Young lady, please get these boys a beverage."

He seemed nice but he couldn't stop looking at the treasure box that Brock had sat on the table.

"Tell me your story, and please, take your time."

We all took our turns telling about our incredible adventure. The moms gasped and the dads grew prouder with every tale. But Brock grew restless and finally said what we had all been thinking.

"Do you want to buy it? How much?"

Rico smiled. "Let's take a look and see the condition."

He slowly and very carefully opened the book and examined it with a magnifying glass.

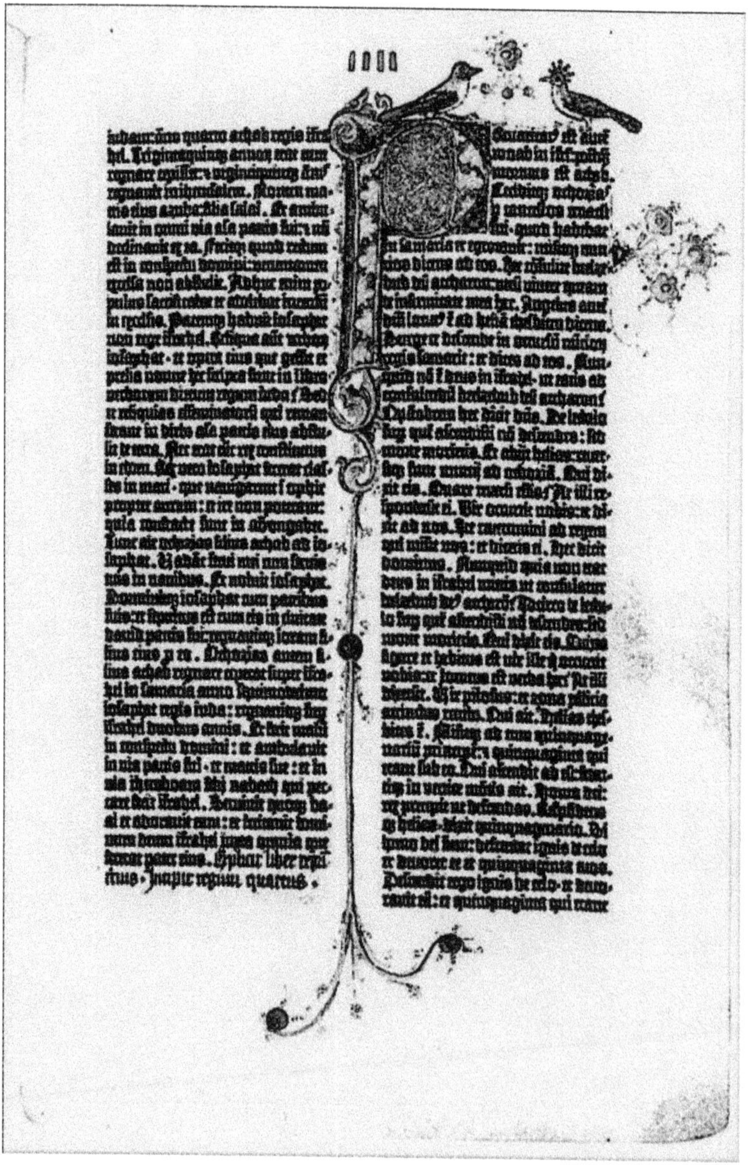

"So my friends, we are in a bit of a quandary here. You haven't had this appraised yet and I'm not certain it's not a forgery. But for the sake of risk verses reward, we both can't wait or time will take away our opportunities. So...there are four of you." He looked at each of us and called our names, "Caleb, Gage, Brock and Cole." I think a fair deal would be 1 million apiece, 4 million for the book. Here are some papers to sign. It says I have 7 days to confirm its validity and, then my men will have the money transferred to each of your bank accounts. Do we have deal?"

You could hear a pen drop. We looked at each other and nodded. I'm in shock, and not really sure what to say.

"Well, Brock, I want to sweeten the deal a little more for you. This last page says I'm going to pay for your mother's hospital bills. I've already made a call to some cardio specialists at Mercy Hospital and they are going to take good care of her for you."

You'd think we would be jumping for joy, but the whole room was crying.

Brock tried to get up and walk toward Rico with his mother in tow, her arms wrapped around his neck. The men stepped forward, but he turned and told them it's ok. With a huge hug from them both Brock whispered, "Thank you, sir."

He sat down next to him and explained. "I wouldn't take anything for the experience of this adventure, but I've certainly learned that it's all worthless if not shared with friends and family."

"What do you mean by that?"

"When I was riding bicycles, jet skis, flying over the lake, sleeping in the boat, paddling down the stream and in the back of that cave in the storm, I felt comforted by the beauty around me. But each of my friends and my mother were always in my thoughts. Then I realized that what I was seeing and feeling must be shared with all of you for me to truly enjoy it. I guess what I'm saying, is I know we'll all grow old someday like the men we met, and I hope we can share the memories of telling stories in the moonlight like we did on the lake."

Rico looked at him with soft admiration. "We are not supposed to shine as bright as the sun," he said. "We were made in His image. His Son, was the only One without sin Who could and did suffer for our gain. Our best life would be to reflect the sun like the moon. To do our best to reflect His goodness to everything around us. The real beauty is that it is your choice. You can be a reflection of the light whether crescent, waxing, or waning. But the most romantic light in the universe that has guided more universal love than any object ever has and always will be a full moon! We are most illuminated when we fully reflect the glory of our Savior so that others see Him shining all around us."

"What are you talking about, Rico? I get that you're rich and I guess now we are, too, but while I'm very grateful, I don't understand what you just said. In fact, I don't understand how that crazy book we found gives us immortality as the story suggested."

"But, young man, that's the most beautiful part of what you found. It's not that it's worth money but you have indeed found the treasure that gives immortality...riches beyond your wildest dreams and it is absolutely free for you and all of your friends. But listening to your stories, I believe what each of you really seek is the unconditional love of a perfect Father. And it is within your grasp."

"Wait," said Brock. "What does that mean?"

"What if I told you that I know your Father, and He left some letters with me to give you."

"You know my father? He gave you letters for me? About what?"

His smile grew and he leaned forward. "They are about how much He loves you and how to be truly happy and have peace in your heart every single day."

Brock's eyes and mouth were wide open. He couldn't speak, and wasn't even sure what to think. "Can...can I see them, please?"

"What if I told you He loved you more than anything in the world. If I gave you these letters would you read them every day?" asked the old man.

"ABSOLUTLEY! Please, sir, can I see them?"

"Please be patient, son! I have them for each of you."

That's when Gage and Cole looked puzzled. And Cole asked, "you also know my father?" He turned around to look at his dad.

"Yes, son. So, these letters are more valuable than any amount of gold or silver!"

He reached into his leather satchel and handed us each small pocket-sized small brown books. "This is the New Testament. It is full of letters divinely inspired by your heavenly Father."

"My what?"

"Please listen, and I tell you a story about these letters and why they were written - and by whom."

We all sat still as he began to explain what we would learn is the greatest adventure story ever.

"What if I told you there are letters and stories in this book with answers to every question you could ever dream of asking? This book sells 100 million copies each year. 50 copies are sold every minute. Its complexity can boggle great minds, and yet its simplicity can be understood by children. It's the most widely read, most fiercely debated, and most often quoted book in history. But it was inspired by your heavenly Father just for you! It holds love letters of wisdom from a Father that loves you even more than you can imagine. It's filled with stories about love, families, and forgiveness, but also battles with swords and spears that bring death and life. The Bible is one book, divided into two major divisions - the Old Testament, which contains 39 separate books, and the New Testament, which contains 27 books. Each of these books is further divided into chapter and verse. The best explanation I have seen comes from the front of my Gideon Bible and says, 'The Bible contains the mind of God, the state of man, the way of salvation, the doom of sinners, and the happiness of believers. Its doctrines are holy, its precepts are binding, its histories are true, and its decisions are immutable. Read it to be wise, believe it to be safe, and practice it to be holy. It contains light to direct you, food to support you, and comfort to cheer you. It is the traveler's map, the pilgrim's staff, the pilot's compass, the soldier's sword, and the Christian's charter. Here paradise is restored, heaven opened and the gates of hell disclosed. Christ is its grand subject, our good, the design, and the glory of God its end. It should fill the memory, rule the heart, and guide the feet. Read it slowly, frequently, and prayerfully. Its a mine of wealth, a paradise of glory, and a river of pleasure. It is given you in life, will be opened at the judgment, and remembered forever. It involves the highest responsibility, will reward the greatest labor, and will condemn all who trifle with its sacred contents.' Now, boys here's the biggest question of all time; if you knew all of this, would you read it?"

"YES, I'm in!"

"Me, too!"

"This is awesome!"

"Yes, it is," said Rico. "But you wouldn't believe how many choose not to. I once had an angry old man tell me how he hated religion and Christians. I asked him why and he started with many questions he already had false answers to for the purpose of trying to prove it wrong. All of them were taken out of context and I was not willing to hang my pearls on the neck of an old boar. So, I made him a deal. I asked him to read the whole Bible and then come back, and I would answer all of his questions. I never heard from him again. We both knew if he read it then certainly his questions would be answered, and he wouldn't need me. But in turn, it would change his life, so I ask you what was he afraid of? Finding truth and real love. His hard heart was so full of fear and he was consumed with angry pride. I bet you can guess why. I've seen the window stickers that state 'No Fear.' But that's much easier said than done. The fear of rejection and failure plague every person as the most common of all fears. It starts with a Father's love. Cole may have fears because he hasn't always been given the love language of positive words of affirmation spoken to like Gage has. But Gage may fear the failure and harsh words of a controlling father who wants his son not to make his own mistakes. You, Brock, think you could be accepted and loved if you just had a father in your life. While all these are real fears in your minds, there is but one solution. To completely accept and understand that the only way to have 'No Fear' is to live and love the one true Father in heaven. So imagine, if what you're doing is not working for you, then search for God's way. When fully consumed with the Holy Spirit you will never ever fail! Realize this, God knows every hair on your head, knows what you are going through and has even allowed you to encounter both rejection and failure for a reason you may never know. When you have this peace in your heart then you will be truly free from the emotions of life that often seem so daunting. Here is the crazy part: even when we are blessed enough to become fathers ourselves, we can't begin to understand our mistakes and failures and the impact it will have on our children. This is when we get valuable lessons in love and forgiveness. Some make it and this is because they were shown how by their fathers, some fake it and this is because they have so many fears of their own they find it hard to lead, and many fail at it because of hard dark hearts from choosing to live a life of pain. But know this, they're all sinners as are you! **For all, 'all not some,' all fall short of the glory of God.** That's in Romans 3:23. **'As it is written, "None are righteous, no not one."'** That's Romans 3:10. See, I thought I knew love until my sons were born, and then I realized that I would give my life in an instant if it meant my sons could live. Imagine, who would you run in front of a train to save? Perhaps your friend, but I'm certain you would think about it first. Perhaps your girlfriend. But this I can promise you - for your own son, you wouldn't blink an eye! You would face death with no fear if it meant saving your son. However, if someone told me that the death of my son would save another, I would not ever want to give it. But what if it saved a thousand? A million? A billion? I would still give it thought, but pray I don't ever have to, because I couldn't or wouldn't want to live without either of my sons. Would you like to be loved by a perfect Father is this way? Then listen to this, God so loved you that He gave His One and only Son, so that if you believe in Him you will have eternal life with Him in heaven! Look it up in John 3:16. 'Eternal,' that's infinite, forever and ever! Imagine a bird uses his beak to pick up a grain of sand from a beach in Kenya and flew across the continent of Africa - which is bigger than the US, Russia, and China combined - then across the Atlantic Ocean to the beaches of the east Texas Coast, then flew back again to get another grain and did this until all the sand from one beach was moved to the other. Would that take an hour, day, week, year, decade, centennial, millennia or a decamillennial in heaven? If time is infinite would it matter? Only if you were in Hell burning in a lake of fire! See, a unit of time is any particular time interval, used as a standard way of measuring or expressing duration. The base unit of time in the International System of Units and by most of the Western world, is defined as about 9 billion oscillations of the Cesium atom. And who created the atom? The first words of seeking wisdom are 'In the beginning God created the heaven and earth,' as read in Genesis 1. So, what do you have to lose? Well, you can reject him and this wisdom, continue to exist as you have been. Perhaps I'm wrong and we die to never exist again, so nothing you do matters. But what if you choose not to study the bible, and ignore this wisdom to finally learn the word is true when it's too late? Then you would spend eternity in hell with weeping and gnashing of teeth, while the righteous shine like the sun in their Father's kingdom, as we read in Matthew 13:41. This is absolutely your choice! As is living a life of peace and love today. **'For the wages of sin is death, but the free gift of God is eternal life in Christ Jesus our Lord.'** That's Romans 6:23. **'For I deliver to you as first importance what I also receive: that Christ died for our sins in accordance with the scriptures, that He was buried, that He was raised on the third day in accordance with the scriptures.'** We find that in 1 Corinthians 15:3-4. **'And then he tells us; behold, I stand at the door and knock. If anyone hears My voice and opens the door, I will come to Him.'** That's Revelation 3:20. **'For everyone who calls on the name of the Lord will be saved.'** We read that in Romans 10:13."

"So that's it?" said Cole. "Just repeat some words and I'm saved?"

"Yes, but that is just the beginning. It's called 'justification.' Join me on our knees and speak these words out loud with me and from deep within your heart: 'Yeshua, my King, Creator of all that is seen and unseen, Maker of my heart. I confess I am a sinner in great need of Your perfect love. I don't deserve Your mercy and can't earn Your grace, but I thank You with all that is within me for the wonderful gift of the forgiveness that You so freely gave us in Your sinless death on the cross, and saved us with Your glorious resurrection. I humbly ask You to come into my heart and be my heavenly Father, forever and ever, Amen!"

"Now, my son, you have received the free gift of salvation. And now comes the wonderful journey of sanctification toward glorification!"

"The what? Ok, I get this faith thing, and I believe, but I don't know anything about religion and not am sure where to go from here."

He smiled and said, "you know, I'm still learning, too."

"But don't I need to be baptized in water or something?"

He smiled again. "Baptism is the outward expression of the decision you already made in your heart. You just made a wonderful choice to become part of a beautiful family that is the body of Christ!"

Brock looked at him with a raised eyebrow, and the old man continued. "Prepare to be tested. Sometimes in my life I've failed miserably as a Christian. What helped me was being part of a good Church - like my biblical mentors, brethren, and family at a small town Church where I was discipled. There was a little girl there named Sophie, well actually I think she was an angel, she would give me a hug on days when I needed it most. Her whole family shined so brightly with the love of God. Ah," he said while looking up. "My Sunday school class that was full of fathers and grandfathers who always made me feel welcome. The wonderful giving volunteers in AWANA like Chrissy, Shelly, Eleanor - just to name a few." Tears came to his eyes as he thought of each one. He paused and smiled with joy. "There are so many more, I can't name them all. My faith journey has taken me down many paths. I've personally have been called Anglican, Baptist, and Methodist. I have even studied Catholicism and attended masses while touring beautiful chapels all over America. My adventures across our great nation has led me to many wonderful words of wisdom from Godly, Spirit-filled leaders leaders like Dr. David Jeremiah of Shadow Mountain Church in El Cajon California and the wonderful theological teachings of Pastor Michael Head very near here in Branson. Let me tell you what I learned about religion, it's not the name on the building. It's the people inside and their beliefs that matter most. Do they believe in the Trinity which is 'the Father, Son and Holy Spirit.' Do they preach from the bible? Do they take scripture out of context? You can't understand a book by reading one page, or understand a paragraph by reading one sentence. When you read a letter, the date is on the top right corner, the signature at the bottom right, and the body in the center. If you want to understand Scripture you read all of it to find who was doing the writing, to whom they were addressing, when, and why. God will reveal truths to you when you stay in His Word. As an example: many non-believers want to do whatever they choose and have no consequences whatsoever will be quick to quote the Bible and tell you that you should not judge. But that's the only part they know. The Bible actually says it differently: that we should hold our brethren accountable to try and keep them from sinning. It's just best when done by a friend who has already overcome the sin and has humbly repented. Clearly, I shouldn't scold or correct you for stealing coins from another if I just stole some as well. Make sense...or 'cents'? Pardon the pun. I had to lighten it up. Listen, it's simple. God is good and does not change. A loving God never tries to control you. You are free to choose. Be careful to remember: **'For the Word of God is alive and active. Sharper than any double-edged sword, it penetrates even to dividing soul and spirit, joints and marrow; it judges the thoughts and attitudes of the heart.'** That's Hebrews 4:12. And my favorite that helped my own faith in my heavenly Father: **'Ask, and it shall be given you; seek, and ye shall find, knock, and it shall be opened unto you. For every one that asketh receiveth, and he that seeketh findeth, and to him that knocketh it shall be opened. Or what man is there of you, whom if his son ask bread, will he give him a stone? Or if he ask a fish, will he give him a serpent? If ye then, being evil, know how to give good gifts unto your children, how much more shall your Father which is in heaven give good things to them that ask Him? Therefore, all things whatsoever ye would that men should do to you, do ye even so to them, for this is the law and the prophets.'"**

"Wow! This is crazy cool!"

"And comforting."

"Da bomb!"

We all laughed.

"We have talked about a lot but... let's get back to this Father stuff."

"Ok Brock, here is what I want you to do. Whenever you want to feel the love of your Father, pick up your Bible and read it. When you want to learn even more and feel great, go somewhere and read it with friends and when you get so excited, share it. Then you will truly know what it is to be rich beyond your wildest dreams! Let me show you...hold it...better yet, you show us. Here, read this aloud to us. John, chapter 14, from verse 1 to 31."

Brock took the Bible and it curved over his hands as he laid it in his lap.

"Let not your heart be troubled: ye believe in God, believe also in Me.

In My Father's house are many mansions: if it were not so, I would have told you. I go to prepare a place for you.

And if I go and prepare a place for you, I will come again, and receive you unto Myself; that where I am, there ye may be also.

And whither I go ye know, and the way ye know.

Thomas saith unto Him, Lord, we know not whither Thou goest; and how can we know the way?

Jesus saith unto him, I am the way, the truth, and the life: no man cometh unto the Father, but by Me.

If ye had known Me, ye should have known My Father also: and from henceforth ye know Him, and have seen Him.

Philip saith unto Him, Lord, show us the Father, and it sufficeth us.

Jesus saith unto him, Have I been so long time with you, and yet hast thou not known Me, Philip? He that hath seen Me hath seen the Father; and how sayest thou then, Show us the Father?

Believest thou not that I am in the Father, and the Father in Me? The words that I speak unto you I speak not of Myself: but the Father that dwelleth in Me, He doeth the works.

Believe Me that I am in the Father, and the Father in Me: or else believe Me for the very works' sake.

Verily, verily, I say unto you, He that believeth on Me, the works that I do shall he do also; and greater works than these shall he do; because I go unto My Father.

And whatsoever ye shall ask in My name, that will I do, that the Father may be glorified in the Son.

If ye shall ask any thing in My name, I will do it.

If ye love Me, keep My commandments.

And I will pray the Father, and He shall give you another Comforter, that He may abide with you for ever;

Even the Spirit of truth; Whom the world cannot receive, because it seeth Him not, neither knoweth Him: but ye know Him; for He dwelleth with you, and shall be in you.

I will not leave you comfortless: I will come to you.

Yet a little while, and the world seeth Me no more; but ye see Me: because I live, ye shall live also.

At that day ye shall know that I am in My Father, and ye in Me, and I in you.

He that hath My commandments, and keepeth them, he it is that loveth Me: and he that loveth Me shall be loved of My Father, and I will love Him, and will manifest Myself to Him.

Judas saith unto him (not Iscariot), Lord, how is it that Thou wilt manifest Thyself unto us, and not unto the world?

Jesus answered and said unto him, If a man love Me, he will keep My words: and My Father will love him, and We will come unto him, and make Our abode with him.

He that loveth Me not keepeth not My sayings: and the word which ye hear is not Mine, but the Father's which sent Me.

These things have I spoken unto you, being yet present with you.

But the Comforter, which is the Holy Ghost, Whom the Father will send in My name, He shall teach you all things, and bring all things to your remembrance, whatsoever I have said unto you.

Peace I leave with you, My peace I give unto you: not as the world giveth, give I unto you. Let not your heart be troubled, neither let it be afraid.

Ye have heard how I said unto you, I go away, and come again unto you. If ye loved Me, ye would rejoice, because I said, I go unto the Father: for My Father is greater than I.

And now I have told you before it come to pass, that, when it is come to pass, ye might believe.

Hereafter I will not talk much with you: for the prince of this world cometh, and hath nothing in Me.

But that the world may know that I love the Father; and as the Father gave Me commandment, even so I do. Arise, let us go hence.

We were all quiet. A tear rolled down Brock's face and landed on the page. He looked up smiling and said, "I started this adventure to help my mother get a new heart. But I also got one, and a Father, a perfect One Who loves me very much. Mr. Rico, will you baptize me in the river below the bridge where we first opened this treasure book?"

"I can do that, if you do something for me."

"Anything. Just ask."

"Bring your friends and family. They will want to share this very special moment together."

We turned to look at our parents behind us, and they were glowing with pride and joy!

"The money will be sent to your father's account, and he will distribute to each of you just as the letter describes. But most significantly, you now have the secret of true wealth and happiness! Let's shine this light brightly and use our testimony to inspire others. Be aware that now you'll be tested, but will gain strength and grow resilient by staying close to your family."

"By family, you mean my mom?" said Brock.

"No. Look around you, these are now your brothers and sisters in Christ. You'll find many more in a good, Bible-based church that will also become your family. I will see you all again very soon. Until then, peace be with you my friends!"

He stood up and reached out to give us a hug, picked up the treasure, and stood next to his guards as they prepared to escort him out the door. We turned to take one long slow last look when Brock said, "What are you thinking now, brother Gage?"

"I think our hearts were blessed to be treasure hunters, and there's still many lost souls and silver out there somewhere!"

"What are you thinking, Brock?"

"Well first, I want to take my treasure money and build a beautiful baptismal pond that resembles the river - maybe with a gentle waterfall that can be seen from a glass-front prayer sanctuary so I can share this wonderful Spirit of God with other adventure travelers!"

"What are you thinking, Cole?"

"I'm thinking it's time for a great meal at this excellent restaurant we're in. I'm buying!"

The whole room was laughing out loud!

Reaching for Maya's hand never felt better. I held it tightly on my right side. I reached over with my left to grab Caleb, who grabbed Brock's, who in turn reached for Cole.

We all leaned toward each other and said with a giggle and a grin, "Let the adventure begin!"

ABOUT THE AUTHOR

Kory Umlauf is a Christian Father, Author, Artist, Foodservice Consultant and Outdoor Adventurer. His creative talents and tenacious desire for knowledge have taken him on many adventures through life. From Executive Chef of Fine Dining Restaurants to a Foodservice Distribution National Account Advisor and Hospitality Consultant to include successful work for a Safari company sending him on incredible wild adventures across Kenya, swimming with Sharks in Southern California and hiking the Grand Canyon. Growing up and living in the beautiful Ozarks trekking its many clear streams, deep lakes and cool caverns he always pursues peaceful prayer while wandering and writing in the wilderness!

www.ingramcontent.com/pod-product-compliance
Lightning Source LLC
Chambersburg PA
CBHW070618310726
48982CB00001B/115